WHAT IF
A FISH

WHAT IF A FISH

Anika Fajardo

SIMON & SCHUSTER BOOKS FOR YOUNG READERS
New York London Toronto Sydney New Delhi

SIMON & SCHUSTER BOOKS FOR YOUNG READERS
An imprint of Simon & Schuster Children's Publishing Division
1230 Avenue of the Americas, New York, New York 10020

SIMON & SCHUSTER BOOKS FOR YOUNG READERS is a trademark of Simon & Schuster, Inc.
For information about special discounts for bulk purchases, please contact Simon & Schuster Special Sales at 1-866-506-1949 or business@simonandschuster.com.
The Simon & Schuster Speakers Bureau can bring authors to your live event. For more information or to book an event, contact the Simon & Schuster Speakers Bureau at 1-866-248-3049 or visit our website at www.simonspeakers.com.
Book design by Lizzy Bromley
The text for this book was set in Adobe Garamond.
Manufactured in the United States of America
0720 BVG
First Edition
10 9 8 7 6 5 4 3 2 1
Library of Congress Cataloging-in-Publication Data
Names: Fajardo, Anika, author.
Title: What if a fish / Anika Fajardo.
Description: First edition. | New York : Simon & Schuster Books for Young Readers, [2020] | Audience: Ages 8-12. | Audience: Grades 4-6. | Summary: "Eleven-year-old Eddie Aguado is convinced that winning the 14th Annual Arne Hopkins Dock Fishing Tournament (once he actually learns how to fish) will bring him closer to his dad, who died when Eddie was only five"— Provided by publisher.
Identifiers: LCCN 2019024567 (print) | LCCN 2019024568 (ebook) | ISBN 9781534449831 (hardcover) | ISBN 9781534449855 (ebook)
Subjects: CYAC: Fathers and sons—Fiction. | Brothers—Fiction. | Grief—Fiction. | Fishing—Fiction. | Colombian Americans—Fiction.
Classification: LCC PZ7.1.F3475 Wh 2020 (print) | LCC PZ7.1.F3475 (ebook) | DDC [Fic]—dc23
LC record available at https://lccn.loc.gov/2019024567
LC ebook record available at https://lccn.loc.gov/2019024568

To Sylvia

1

THE WATER by the shore smells like the bottom of the garbage pail right after I take out the trash. I scrunch up my nose and head down the wooden boards of the T-shaped dock. A dad with a small child points across the lake, while a man in a dirty Twins cap blasts country music from an old radio. Leaning my elbows on the dock's railing, I watch the gray-green fish dart and glide below me.

"What are you doing?" asks a loud voice. It's the purple-haired girl I noticed at day camp this morning.

"Quiet," I say. "You'll scare the fish."

"Oh, and that thing won't?" She nods her chin toward the radio.

She has a point.

"Look." She leans close—too close—and points at a flyer stapled to the dock next to where I'm resting my elbows.

The flyer has a picture of a smiling fish fishing. A speech bubble coming out of its mouth says, *Catch me if you can!*

I recognize that fish from somewhere.

"What is it?" the girl asks, as if I know.

"I'm not sure—" I start to say. But then I realize I *am* sure. "It's a fishing contest."

"You're right." She taps the words on the paper and reads aloud, "'The Fourteenth Annual Arne Hopkins Dock Fishing Tournament. Enter for your chance to win the five-thousand-dollar prize.'" She whistles through teeth that stick out like a bunny's. "That's a lot of cash. Who's Arne Hopkins?"

"No idea. I never heard of him until a couple of weeks ago when I found this."

I pull a smooth disc out of my pocket. It's a medal—orangish pink, like it's trying to be bronze. Third place. On one side is a picture of the same smiling fish holding a fishing rod, and the words "2nd Annual Arne Hopkins Dock Fishing Tournament" are squeezed in around the circle.

The girl leans in, and I realize that her hair isn't completely purple, just the ends. Most of it's blond, making her look kind of like a sunset. She grabs the medal from my hand and flips it over. I don't need to look at it to know that it says *Eduardo Aguado León* in faded engraved script.

"Who's Eduardo Aguado León?" she asks, mutilating the pronunciation.

"My dad."

"Your dad won this contest?" The girl stares at me like I'm giving away the secrets of the universe.

"I suppose." I don't feel the need to tell her that I barely remember him, much less know if he really won some fishing tournament.

"You going to enter?" she asks, handing me back the medal.

I snap my fingers shut around the disc. "It says you have to have a team—at least two people."

"Why don't you and your dad enter?"

I ignore her question. Instead I say, more to myself than to her, "If Liam were still here, he would've been my partner. But he just moved away."

"I don't know who Liam is, but you're in luck," the girl says. She squints her eyes and places one hand behind her back and the other flat against her stomach. She isn't smiling, but she winks at me as she bows deeply at the waist. "I guess I moved to Minnesota just in time. I'll be your partner." Upright again, she holds out her hand like a grown-up. "Pleased to meet you. I'm Cameron."

I look at her hand. The nails are bitten down, and her wrist has a stain of green marker, probably from the nametag decorating we had to do this morning. Kamp Kids day camp—also known as summer day care—is just as pointless as I thought it would be. This morning we were forced to play name games in big circles. I wasn't in Cameron's group. Then we ate our bag lunches under trees while getting dive-bombed by flies. I'm desperately counting the minutes until my half brother arrives from Colombia and I don't have to go to camp anymore. Just seven more days.

"Well?" Cameron is looking at me expectantly. "Aren't

you going to tell me your name? That's what people do, you know."

"People call me—" I decide I don't want to tell her what people call me. "Eddie," I say, because it's true. Short for Edward Aguado. Like my dad's name, only different. Our names aren't the only things that make us different.

She squints at me. "Where are you from, Eddie?"

"Here."

"No. Where are you—"

"Like I said, here. Minneapolis," I interrupt. "What grade are you in?"

"Going into sixth. Starting Central Middle School in the fall."

"Me too," I say.

She pulls a phone out of her jeans pocket and snaps a picture of the flyer. I wish I had a phone. My mom and her rules.

"I went to Catholic school before," Cameron says as if I had asked her. "Yep. Moving from California. Switching to public school. Life is really something, isn't it?"

As a matter of fact, it really is. I pat my pocket where Papa's medal is safely tucked away. Two weeks ago I'd never heard of the Arne Hopkins Dock Fishing Tournament, and now I've seen it twice.

"What do you say?" Cameron puts her phone away. "We should enter. What do we have to lose? Don't you want to win five thousand dollars?"

Five thousand dollars? Last week the repair shop told Mama that something needed to be replaced in her car.

Something expensive. I don't know what. She asked how long she could wait to fix the Honda. "You got a couple months, sweetheart," the mechanic said. She rolled her eyes. She hates when people talk to her like that.

"Twenty-five hundred each." Cameron slaps the flyer.

Two thousand five hundred dollars sure would help. I bet that would be enough for the mechanic to fix Mama's Honda.

"What do you say, Eddie? Partners?"

My fingers grip the medal in my pocket. I think of Papa. What if I could win a medal just like he did?

"Let's fish," I say.

2

THERE'S ONLY one problem: I don't know how to fish. As we walk back from the lake, I find out that Cameron doesn't either.

"I'm not saying I've *never* fished," she says. "Because I have. Once."

I wonder if I ever went fishing. If I did, I don't remember.

"Before my parents split up," she adds, her voice low.

I want to ask what happened after they split, but she changes the subject, saying, "It can't be that hard." She hangs her arms down at her sides and starts walking like an orangutan. "I smart. I catch fish. How about you?"

I hang my arms down too. "I catch fish." We laugh and make monkey sounds and jump around like a couple of goofballs. Then we run to catch up with the other Kamp Kids campers heading back to the Lake Madeline Rec Center.

As we follow them, the straggly line reminds me of Little Tykes Preschool, where all the toddlers used to hold knots in a rope during walking field trips. And that reminds me of the day when Mama's friend Sarah picked me up while I was playing with the plastic whales at the water table. I remember I didn't want to leave.

While we wait for our rides home at the end of the day, Cameron clicks to the flyer picture on her phone and we look at the rules again. We have a week to pay the entrance fee and six weeks to get ready to win.

"What about the money for entering the tournament?" she asks. "Do you know where we can get fifty bucks?"

"No." I practically have to shout because now that the counselors have decided they're not in charge of us anymore, four of the Kamp Kids boys have started a wrestling match and the second-grade girls run in circles around me and Cameron like we don't even exist. "That's a lot of money."

The horn of a burgundy sedan honks from the street, and Cameron waves. "That's my dad," she says. "We'll think of something." She holds her hand above her eyebrow in a salute.

"What about fishing poles?" I call after her.

"They're called rods," she yells as she climbs into the car. Two small heads bob up and down in the backseat. "Fishing rods. We'll need those, too."

So, it turns out there are three problems: I don't know how to fish, I don't have fifty bucks, and I don't have a fishing pole—I mean, rod. I toss the three things around in my brain. Which to worry about first?

· ✳ · ✳ ·

That night I ask Mama about the fifty dollars I need to enter the contest to win the money and a medal of my own. "Can I have fifty bucks?"

"Set the table." She concentrates on the carrots and green onions she's chopping for our salad.

It was worth a try.

I get two forks out of the drawer. "Do you know *how* I can get fifty bucks?" I say.

"Most of us earn our money."

Mama just got her RN license—that stands for "registered nurse"—and a good job at the hospital, so she's feeling pretty proud right now. Her new salary is the whole reason we could move out of the rotten apartment and into our house. Well, not a house, a duplex. (Someone else lives on the other side of the two one-car garages.) But since I always lived in an apartment before now, the duplex feels like a mansion to me. It has a front and back yard, space for Mama's art supplies, a garage for her car (and all our stuff), and three bedrooms—one for me, one for her, and one for my half brother, who arrives next week.

"We need knives, too," she adds.

"Okay. I'll make a deal with you," I say as I lay the forks and knives on the folded paper towels we use for napkins. "I'll do extra chores; you pay me."

"What does a kid need fifty dollars for?" Mama looks at me and smiles. She runs her fingers through her short blond hair, and a carrot shaving gets stuck in it.

I reach up and brush the shaving out. "Did Papa fish when he was a kid in Colombia?"

The kitchen goes as quiet as the hospital room was the day Papa had his heart attack. Mama slops whole-wheat spaghetti into two bowls and then sets the salad on the table.

I sit down before I say anything else. "Did he?" My voice is as tiny as a pebble.

She sits down. She lifts her fork. Then she puts it down like she can't decide what to do. "Colombia has amazing fish. Huge ones, little ones, colorful ones. I used to see stingrays and the shadows of jellyfish when the waves landed on the beach." She closes her eyes and takes a bite of spaghetti smothered in the green sauce she likes so much.

I look at my plate. This is how it always is. Mama talks about Colombia—where Papa was from and where my half brother lives—but she won't really talk *about* my dad. Eduardo Aguado León. He had two last names because that's what people have in Colombia. One is their father's and one is their mother's. It makes sense to be named after both parents, if you think about it. After all, I have my dad's black hair and brown eyes and my mom's short fingers and small nose. My skin is a mixture of both of them, the color of the coffee ice cream Mama orders at the concessions stand by the lake.

Later that night, while I'm reading about boats in the B volume of my encyclopedia, Mama comes into my room.

"How long have we lived here? Two weeks?" She sits on the edge of the bed. "Now it's summer and we still haven't unpacked everything, much less organized."

I lean against her warm shoulder. We moved the week before school got out. Last year I stayed at Liam's for most of the summer, but now that he and his sister and mom have moved to New York, it's Kamp Kids for me, like everyone else whose parents won't let them stay home alone. But I only have to do it for one more week. Until my brother gets here.

"The garage is a disaster. If you tell me what you need the money for, I'll let you earn it by organizing in there."

"The money is just an entrance fee for a contest. For me and . . . someone I met at camp." I'm embarrassed to admit it's a girl.

"What kind of contest?" She sounds suspicious.

I don't tell her the name of the fishing tournament. She doesn't know I have Papa's medal. I found it when we were packing to move, and I'm afraid it'll make her sad, like when she found her sketchbook. The book was in a long-forgotten storage box at the apartment, and when she saw it, she immediately sat down crisscross-applesauce on the floor of her bedroom and pored through the drawings, as if she weren't the person who'd sketched them in the first place. There was one she had drawn of me as a toddler sleeping on the ratty floral couch we used to have, and drawings of vases with flowers, swirling seashells, hands and fingers. When she turned to the last page, she gasped. It was an unfinished sketch of Papa lying on the rumpled sheets of the hospital bed. Half of his face was drawn with her neat, even lines and shaded with a charcoal smudge. The other half was just a faint sketch, almost like he was disappearing, even then. Mama cried so hard that day, her tears left blots on the drawing. I hugged her with all my might, but there wasn't anything I could do to make her stop.

"It's a fishing contest," I tell her now.

"A fishing contest? But you hate fishing."

"I've never been fishing," I say.

"Yes, you have," Mama says. "Your dad took you when you were little. You and your brother when he visited one summer. You were probably, what, three years old? Or not quite. But you hated it."

I shake my head. "At the dock? I would remember that," I say. I want to hold up my hand like people do when they want the other person to stop talking.

"Not the dock. It was at a friend's cabin. Papa's friend from graduate school, great guy. Anyway, they took you out on a boat. You cried the whole time, he told me, from the moment the worm went onto the hook." She knocks her shoulder against mine again. "I can't imagine you in a fishing contest." Then she laughs at me.

Moms aren't supposed to laugh at their kids, but they do sometimes. The way Mama is laughing at me now reminds me of when Liam and I let his little sister, Clara, play video games with us. She could never get the hang of moving her avatar around. She was always stuck staring at the sky or at her own feet. Liam would grab her controller until he got her situated again. And we would laugh at her because she was cute and also clueless. That's how Mama is laughing at me now.

"If you want to do it, though, I'm happy to help. Papa's poles are probably in the garage somewhere."

She gives me a sideways squeeze that reminds me of that day when I was in preschool. When Mama's friend dropped me off at the hospital, Mama was waiting for me at the entrance. She hugged me as if I were going to float away and it was her last chance to hang on.

"They're called rods," I say.

"Okay, rods. Maybe your brother can fish with you when he gets here." My half brother is going to live with us while he takes classes at the university, a special summer school program for people like him, students from other countries. He's studying bioengineering just like Papa did.

I think of Papa's fishing gear somewhere in the garage. I think of my brother. "Do you suppose he knows how to fish?"

"You'll have to ask him yourself," she says, standing up.

"And if we win, Mama, we can fix your car."

"Don't worry about my car," she says, even though she knows I will because I worry about a lot of things. I worry about our cat that ran away three years ago. I worry about not having a best friend in middle school since Liam moved away. I worry about whether my brother will want to hang out with me.

The one thing I'm not worried about right now is winning a medal of my own.

3

I DON'T KNOW what kind it will be, but I am going to catch a big fish. The biggest fish. And I'll win that award. The money. The medal. It'll be perfect.

I'm telling Cameron this the next day as we walk toward Lake Madeline with the other campers. When we get to the lake, the Kamp Kids counselors hand out cups of lemonade, and a bunch of kids start dumping it on each other. While the teenagers are busy trying to stop the mayhem, Cameron and I sneak onto the dock again. She slips her nametag inside her T-shirt, and I do the same—being in day camp when you're eleven is embarrassing enough without the nametags.

"Guess what? My mom is going to pay us to clean the garage," I tell her. "Earn the money for the tournament fee."

"Really? Me too? Your mom doesn't even know me."

It's true that Mama doesn't know Cameron, but then again, I never had many friends other than Liam. Mama has been best friends with Liam's mom since before me and Liam were born. He and I have known each other forever, but now . . . now that he moved away, I don't know if we're going to always stay best friends.

Right before Liam, Clara, and Sarah packed up their moving truck to leave for New York, he and I were in his room sitting between all the cardboard boxes—his collection of stuffed penguins, his Xbox, even the skateboard that he was so bad at riding, were getting packed. Clara ran in and out of the room, yelling "Boo!" each time. Sometimes she's the cutest little girl ever, and sometimes she makes me so glad I don't have a sister.

Liam couldn't stop talking about New York and the new stepdad and stepbrothers he would have. I couldn't stop staring at the dust bunnies and a teddy-bear-shaped button caught under a baseboard.

"The older one, Enrique, he's going into eighth grade, so we'll be at the same school. And Pedro is seven, almost the same as Clara."

"Will you ride the bus to school?" I asked Liam, thinking of our hideout in between the dark green seats of the Minneapolis school bus. Ever since kindergarten we'd been riding the same bus to and from school.

"No, man. We walk," he said with a different rhythm to his words. He never used to say "man" like that. "Isn't that cool?"

He shimmied under the bed and dug around like he was

a paleontologist. Then he popped back out, his shirt coated in dust.

"Got it!" he announced, holding up a plastic bronto-saurus.

"The kids are Puerto Rican?" I asked.

Liam nodded, his cowlick of reddish-blond hair bobbing. "Super cool. They already taught me some Spanish curse words." Liam leaned against the bed and picked at something pink on the dinosaur's feet. "They're so cool, not like all the boring Minnesotans in this neighborhood."

If Liam's mirror hadn't already been covered in Bubble Wrap, I would've looked at myself. "What about me?" I asked.

"What about you?"

"I'm Colombian." I stood up and brushed the grime from the butt of my jeans.

"Well, not really, Eddie," he said, tucking the dinosaur into his pocket. "You're not *Colombian* Colombian."

"My dad was. And that makes me half-Colombian."

"But you don't speak Spanish."

He was right. I don't speak Spanish.

"But," I said, "my brother does."

"That's cool. You have your Colombian half brother, and then you have me. We're brothers for life, right?"

He stood up and held out his fist, ready for me to bump it.

I looked at my best friend's hand with its freckles and the scar on the right thumb from when we fell off the sled last winter, and the nick on his pinkie from when he cut himself on a root beer can. I knew him. Or at least I thought

I did. And I thought he knew me. But then how could he say I wasn't Colombian? Papa. My brother. They were both Colombian without any doubt. Is it true that just because I don't speak Spanish, I can't be Colombian?

"I gotta go," I said, and left Liam's fist hanging in the air like a fish out of water.

That was the last time I saw him. And now I don't know if we're still friends.

Either way, the fact is that Liam is in New York and Cameron is here.

"My mom says if we do a good job cleaning the garage, we get fifty bucks," I tell her. "If we do a bad job, we owe her ten each."

Cameron laughs. "I am at your service." She places one sneaker-clad foot behind the other and slowly bends her knees. It might be a curtsy, but it's hard to tell when the girl doing the curtsy is wearing jean shorts. "What about fishing poles?" she asks.

"You mean rods?"

She laughs. "Rods. Right."

"We're in luck there, too, because my mom says we have rods somewhere in the garage."

"It's going to be perfect," Cameron says, and I hope she's right.

We both lean on the dock's splintery railing and listen to the shouts of the counselors onshore.

"What are you going to do with the prize money?" I ask.

"Visit my mom."

"Where is she?"

"San Francisco, where we used to live." She pulls at a sliver of the gray railing. The wood is golden brown underneath. I'm worried she's going to get a splinter in her finger if she keeps doing that.

"Who do you live with?"

"My dad."

She says the word "dad" like it's the most ordinary, boring word in the world. Like a dad is something as tedious as a broom or a frying pan. I gaze into the murky lake water. What's down there below the surface?

"Can't your dad take you to San Francisco?" I ask.

She grunts but doesn't answer. I glance back at the kids on the shore. They're playing another circle game in the shade. One of the counselors watches us while thumbing at her phone. A girl whose sparkly earrings hang to her shoulders is walking onto the dock. She's holding a pink ice cream cone, and she looks familiar. As she gets closer to us, I can see that the ice cream is strawberry. And that the girl is Alyssa Schmidt. I don't like Alyssa or her two rotten older brothers. She stops a few feet away and pretends she doesn't see us.

"Nice bling, huh?" Cameron whispers to me.

"She's super popular," I whisper back. "At school."

We watch her as she licks her ice cream.

"Hey," Alyssa says when she catches us staring. Her eyes flick to Cameron's purple hair and untied Converse sneakers.

"How do you do?" Cameron asks like she's someone's great-aunt.

"Are you new?" Alyssa's not talking to me. We've been in the same class every year since second grade. Just my luck. Maybe I'll escape her in middle school.

"I am new to Minneapolis but old to the world," Cameron says. "I've been around the sun eleven times." She spins around in a circle, and I can't help laughing at her serious expression. Alyssa raises her eyebrows.

Just then, a boy with bright yellow sneakers makes a splash as he falls into the weedy water at the shore. Two of the counselors wade in after him. Alyssa rolls her eyes. "Can you imagine having to go to Kamp Kids? I mean, I used to go when I was little." Alyssa makes a face like she just tasted expired milk.

Cameron and I exchange glances, and my stomach clenches. I'm glad our nametags are hidden. And I'm glad I only have six more days until my brother gets here. No more day care—I mean camp—after that.

"So, mate," Cameron says, this time in an Australian accent, "what are you doing this fine afternoon?"

"Hanging," Alyssa says, her earrings tinkling as she shrugs her shoulders.

I look around. The only thing hanging right now is the lure from the line of a guy fishing down the dock from us.

"What's your name?" Alyssa asks. But before Cameron can be a smart aleck, Alyssa's strawberry ice cream comes loose and tumbles into the greenish water.

We lean over the railing.

"Whoa."

If a cluster of fish is called a school, what appears out

of the lake's depths is less like a classroom and more like a raucous recess. The fish are all different sizes. Big ones, little ones. Iridescent and dull-colored, brown and gold, shiny and scaly. Some have rounded faces, and others are sharp and pointy. So many fish. These are the fish I'm going to catch to win the medal. I try to count them, but they dive at the ice cream, butting one another out of the way in a frantic food fight. They crowd together like squirmy kindergartners.

"Fish eat ice cream?" Alyssa asks, holding her empty sugar cone.

Cameron and I laugh. Hiccup. Alyssa gives a half-hearted chuckle too, even though I'm pretty sure she has no idea what's funny. Actually, I don't know what's so funny either, but Cameron and I can barely stand up, we're laughing so hard. While we're giggling, a berry breaks free from the blob of ice cream, and three fish battle for it. The red lump lurches and jerks from one greedy mouth to another. Alyssa is sort of shrieking now, and Cameron and I are still laughing. The other fishermen on the dock swarm just like the fish, straining to see what we're going on about.

And then we all see it.

"Look at . . . ," Cameron says.

"What is . . . ," Alyssa starts to say.

Everyone on the dock falls silent.

A monster. It can't possibly be a fish. Its mouth is more than twice as big as the other fish crowded around the ice cream. Its angry jaws look like a shark's. Of course, I know there are no sharks in the lakes of Minnesota. But when the creature opens that mouth, snapping its teeth, I have to wonder.

The ice cream is gone in one gulp. The other fish scatter as the beast sinks lower and lower until the only evidence of the whole thing is the pink cloudy water below us. Cameron's mouth is open as wide as that fish's.

My chest swells with anticipation, with hope. What if I can catch *that* fish?

4

THE BIGGEST FISH ever caught in Minnesota was a seventy-eight-inch sturgeon. I tell Cameron this as we fiddle with the lock on the garage door. "That's six feet, six inches." Taller even than my nineteen-year-old brother.

Cameron grins. "You've been Googling fish?" she asks, elbowing me. "Me too. Then you know that sturgeons don't live in the lakes in Minneapolis. You won't catch that on the dock. Muskies, that's what you want."

Muskies. Technically called muskellunge. In the L-M volume of my encyclopedia, I read that a muskellunge is a type of pike. My encyclopedia has every fact you could ever need. I found the set of twelve volumes with glossy pictures and gold edges when we were packing to move. The thing about moving is that you find things you didn't even know you had. Some of the things Mama and I found were sad, like the sketchbook, but some were cool, like the striped T-shirt I thought I'd lost, and the painting of a parrot I did in second grade. And Papa's medal.

When I found the set of encyclopedias in a box tucked behind the rain jackets, snow boots, and an old Candy Land game, Mama didn't want me to keep them. "I don't think we need these. You know, with the internet."

But when I saw the books, I just had to have them. I'm not sure why. I wrote my name on the box in thick black marker. Then, the week before summer vacation, Mama hired a guy and rented a truck while I was at school, and everything—including the encyclopedias—got moved into the new duplex. The set is pretty old, but Wikipedia has nothing on these books. You just open one of them up and learn something you never knew before.

"That monster we saw was a muskie for sure," Cameron says. "Someone caught one that was, like, fifty-seven inches. That's four-foot-nine—just a little shorter than me." She looks at me. "About your height."

Even at four-foot-nine, I can still yank open the garage door. Cameron makes a face as the pulley screeches.

"It's a mess in here, Eddie," she says.

She's right. The garage is so filled with junk, Mama has to park her car outside in the driveway. Boxes stacked two and three high make a lopsided skyline. Mama's old canvases, most of them painted over with white house paint, are propped along one wall behind a mechanical lawn mower, the kind without an engine. There's a big red cooler on wheels that Mama used to bring to the beach at Lake Mad when I was little. There are bottles of blue windshield wiper fluid, and yellow ones filled with the coolant Mama has to keep adding to the car. A microwave sits on the cement floor waiting for its next bag of popcorn. Along one wall is a row of empty metal shelves, where all this stuff needs to go.

"That's why we're getting fifty bucks for organizing it," I say, stooping over the nearest box. "Keep an eye out for fishing gear. My mom says it might be in here."

"Ten-four," Cameron says, opening a box at her feet. "That means 'okay' if you're on a shortwave radio."

In Spanish "okay" is "vale." I learned that from my brother, who called last night. He and Mama talked about when we were going to pick him up from the airport and when his university orientation is. Five more days until he arrives, and I can't wait. When Mama handed me the phone, I told him that we're going to go fishing.

"You know how to fish, right?" I asked. I didn't tell him about the tournament, because I want to surprise him.

"*Sure,*" he said in English. *"I'll see you in one week."*

"Okay." I couldn't tell if he was as excited as I was.

"Say it in Spanish," he said. *"Say 'vale.'"*

"Ball-eh," I repeated.

"Eso." I could hear the smile in his voice. I can't wait for him to get here. For him to help me fish, to hang out.

"Yours?" Cameron holds up a pair of little green mittens connected by a string of green yarn.

"Mine," I say, taking them from her and slinging the string over my shoulders.

"What's the string for?" she asks.

"The string goes through your coat sleeves. Didn't you have mittens like this?"

"I lived in California, remember? No snow?"

"Right. Well, it's a good invention. The string keeps you from losing one of your mittens. Keeps the two of them together."

These are the mittens Liam's mom, Sarah, left in my cubby at Little Tykes Preschool the day she drove me to the hospital. I sat in the backseat of her car, pressing my palm against the cold window and watching the brown and red leaves whip past the spaces between my fingers. It's funny the things you remember.

"This goes here, then." Cameron heaves the box of mittens and scarves onto the shelf near the door. She moves on to another carton. "This whole box is baby clothes," she says. "Why is your mom saving all this stuff? Is she planning on having another baby?"

I shake my head. "My dad died when I was little."

I don't tell her about the sharp smell in the hospital corridors. I don't tell her about holding Mama's hand or about not recognizing the man under the smooth white sheets. Until I saw his mustache. Eduardo Aguado León always wore a thick mustache. I reach into my pocket and make a fist around Papa's medal.

"Oh," she says, in that quiet, respectful way people do. She looks down at the box, avoiding my eyes. We let a silence sit between us.

When Liam and I were seven, we were in his room playing with his *Star Wars* Lego set. I had the Luke Skywalker minifigure and said that Luke had a dead dad just like me and Liam.

"But Luke's dad isn't dead. At least, he doesn't die until later," Liam said, rummaging through the box for a Stormtrooper head to go with its white body. "He's just on the Dark Side."

I knelt next to Liam on the floor, searching for a lightsaber.

"Found it." He shoved a helmet onto his minifigure. "Have you seen a blaster?"

"It's in there. At the bottom."

Liam started digging again. "Anyway, my dad isn't dead either," he added.

I gripped the plastic Jedi and listened to the crackly sound of Legos hitting each other as Liam dumped bricks onto the floor.

"Aha!" he said, holding up the blaster and snapping it into the Stormtrooper's hand. "My dad lives in Chicago, remember? I just never see him. Like Luke never sees his dad."

I knew that but had forgotten. I looked at Luke and wished I could find his lightsaber. He needed something to protect himself.

"Here, Eddie. Luke's saber." Liam held out the little plastic sword to me. An offering.

Now I watch Cameron drag a cardboard box across the garage. Would she give me a lightsaber if I needed one? I shake my head, trying to empty it of such a silly idea. Cameron and I don't need lightsabers; we need to win the fishing tournament.

Cameron wipes her hands on her shorts. "I have two stepsisters," she says. "Two and five. It's not fun."

I think of Clara as a two-year-old banging spoons on pots and pans in Liam's kitchen while our moms drank coffee. Then my memory is interrupted by the whining siren sound Cameron is making. She's opened another box and is holding up a sweater knitted with five different colors of yarn. "Call the fashion police!" she hollers.

I stumble around the junk. The box she opened is filled with other clothes too, but these are bigger than my baby stuff. Out-of-style men's clothes. Papa's clothes, folded, packed away, as if he'll wear them again. There's a winter coat, one gray T-shirt. A pair of leather work boots caked in ancient mud reminds me of my fourth-grade field trip digging for fossils. It was at a county park where they let kids search for treasures in the shale and sandstone. Alyssa found a rock with the imprint of a leaf, but she threw it into the woods when everyone wanted to see it. Liam discovered a portion of a snail shell fossil in a chunk of sandstone, its perfect curves clearly visible once the dust was brushed away. I almost never push, but I shoved kids aside trying to see the fossils. For some reason, I felt desperate to see the bits of rock that had been there—hidden—in the ground for thousands of years, just waiting to be found.

"I don't know why my mom keeps this junk," I say. I picture Mama crying after she found the sketchbook. Her sadness hangs around her like something you can touch. It's like the paint she sometimes gets on her elbows. Mama can't see the red and black stains, but if you know where to look, you can find them. Maybe when I win the tournament, I'll be able to wash away a little of that sadness.

"We'll put this box on the bottom shelf." Cameron drags the box over and slides it in next to the box of baby clothes. "A place for everything; everything in its place. That's what my dad says."

If everything has its place, why do I feel like I don't know where I fit?

We work in silence for a while. Slowly the boxes from the middle of the garage are lined up on the metal shelves, fitted in like in a game of Tetris. The microwave, an old stereo that probably doesn't work, Mama's canvases.

"Who knew working for fifty bucks would be so much work?" Cameron says from the back corner of the garage.

"It'll be worth it," I remind her. She peeks around a stack of boxes, and her eyes squish into a smile. Is she thinking about that plane ride to visit her mom?

As we work, I try to speed up the process by stacking multiple boxes, so I don't have to take as many trips across the greasy stains on the floor. My arms are piled with three shoeboxes. After opening about a million to see what was in them, we gave up on that. I have no idea what's in these, and I don't really care right now.

"I'm exhausted. Beat. Worn out." Cameron wipes her forehead with the back of her hand.

"Well," I say, grinning, "whatever it takes to win."

And that's when I trip on a rake. The three boxes tumble, their contents scattering across the concrete. Photographs everywhere. The mixed-up jumble on the floor reminds me of a collage I once made in art class. Dozens of pictures cut out of magazines. Compared to the paintings Mama creates, the hodgepodge of images didn't look like much, but my art teacher liked it. He said it was greater than the sum of its parts.

I kneel on the floor. The colors in the pictures are faded, the edges curled. The faces are blurry, and the clothes on the smiling people are as out-of-date as the clothes in these boxes. There's a picture of my brother when he was a little younger than I am now. He's wearing a navy blazer and tie—a Colombian school uniform. Another of him about my age, skinny and scowly in front of a palm tree. (Imagine living in a place with palm trees.) There's Papa with his thick mustache, an arm around Mama. She smiles at the camera, looking exactly like she does now, blond and blue-eyed. She wears her painting smock, the one with drips and splotches. I used to look for ducks and fish and giraffes in the paint stains, like some people do with clouds. In another picture, a dark woman with black hair to her waist holds a roly-poly baby—my half brother and his mom. And there he is in Papa's arms. My dad looks super young, but I can still tell it's him.

"Jackpot!" Cameron suddenly shouts from the back corner. "Found them!"

I scoop the photographs into a pile. From behind a rusty spade and a faded red snow shovel, she pulls out two fishing poles. Rods.

Papa's fishing gear. The gear that got him third place in the dock fishing tournament.

"Entrance fee *and* rods." She holds them out like two dusty swords. "Mission accomplished."

I scramble to my feet, dropping photographs back into the shoebox. But one catches my eye, and I plop down again.

In this picture my brother is no more than four or five years old. Next to him is Papa with that mustache. Between Papa and my brother is the biggest fish I have ever seen. The creature, nose to tail, is at least as tall as the boy in the picture. The fish's eyes look to be about as big as golf balls. The fins are shiny, rainbowlike. The fish doesn't look happy, but both the people in the photograph wear identical, ridiculous smiles on their faces, like they're superheroes or something.

"Now *that* is a fish," Cameron says, leaning over my shoulder with the rods held like crutches.

I flip the picture over, and on the back, written in faint pencil, are the names *Eduardo + Eduardo*. I run my finger over the letters.

"That's my brother, Eddie. And my dad."

"Wait." Cameron shifts both fishing rods to one arm and takes the picture out of my hands. "Eddie? You're both Eddie?"

"My dad was too." I hold out my hand, and she lays the photograph on my palm.

Cameron whistles. "Wild. How do they tell you apart?"

"Promise not to laugh?"

She tilts her head, and I decide that means she's promising.

"Well," I say, sliding the picture into my back pocket, "my brother is Big Eddie and I'm Little Eddie."

She shakes her head and laughs even though she sort of promised not to. "No."

"It's true."

She squints her eyes like she's studying me. "Little Eddie, you need your own name."

"What I need," I say, grabbing the rods—my dad's fishing rods—from her, "is to win that tournament."

5

THE NEXT DAY, after Kamp Kids, I want to go back to the fishing dock, but Mama won't let me go alone unless I promise to wear a life vest. Unfortunately for me, it just so happens that we found one in the garage along with an old green metal box that Cameron said was a tackle box.

"I'll look like a dork," I complain to Mama. I regret ever telling her about the life jacket. I didn't tell her about the photo of Papa and Big Eddie and the fish. I just tucked it into the pages of the X-Y-Z volume of my encyclopedia.

"If you want to go by yourself . . ." She trails off because she knows that I know what she means. She's not budging. We both watch a chickadee flit to the bird feeder we hung outside the kitchen window the first morning we were here. I held the step stool and Mama screwed in the bracket.

"But—" I try. Two more chickadees join the first one.

They chirp in carefree voices like they have no worries.

"Life vest, or no more dock visits without supervision, Little Eddie." She folds her arms in front of her chest to let me know she's not changing her mind.

I groan silently. Only four more days until Big Eddie gets here.

As long as I have to wear the life vest, I decide to bring a fishing rod. I don't exactly know what to do with the assortment of hooks, lines, and eyeless wooden fish I found in the tackle box, so I leave it behind. I wear the vest unzipped and rest the rod on my shoulder.

On the way to the lake, I have to be careful not to poke anyone. There are moms with strollers and dads out jogging. Evening commuters on bikes weave around the slower traffic. Minneapolis is famous for its parks. Almost everyone in this city lives within a ten-minute walk of a park. And the walk to Lake Madeline is only seven minutes from our new duplex. People call it Lake Mad for short. Mad Lake. "Mad" can mean "angry" but it can also mean "crazy," and today, like most summer days, the sidewalk around Lake Mad is filled with goofy-looking Rollerbladers, teenagers with nose piercings, and groups of women who appear to be doing yoga while walking.

Even though the path is busy, the only person on the dock is a black-haired man with his black-haired kid. The kid looks too little to understand what they're doing—much younger than Big Eddie was in that photo with the fish. When Big Eddie gets here, I have a lot to ask him. About the photo. About fishing. Everything I need to know to win the tournament. And get a medal just like Papa's.

The man packs up his gear while his toddler runs around on stubby legs. After they leave, I lean on the railing where I first met Cameron. This time, instead of taking the medal out of my pocket, I hold the fishing rod over the water. Now, I know I can't catch fish without a hook. But I want to see what it feels like to stand on the dock with my own rod.

I rest it in a little notch on the railing and imagine the tournament day: sunny skies, crowds of people, an announcer booming out the entries over a loudspeaker. *And the winner, with the biggest fish, is . . .* The announcer's voice will be deep and low, and the other fishermen will start cheering and clapping before he even says my name. *Edward Aguado!*

"Nice life jacket," a voice says, and my daydream vanishes.

I turn and see two teenage boys, their hair dirty blond and curly. They're on bikes, feet on the boards of the dock, forearms resting on the handlebars. Alyssa's brothers. The Schmidt boys. Behind them, Alyssa straddles a sparkly turquoise bike and plays with her earrings.

"Scared of falling in?" The older one, Mason Schmidt, makes cooing, baby noises.

"Isn't that your boyfriend, Alyssa?" the younger one, Ivan, asks.

"Shut up," she says, and doesn't look at me.

"What's your name, dork?" Mason sneers.

I just keep my head down.

"Alyssa," he says. "What's your boyfriend's name?"

"Eddie. People call him Little Eddie."

Mason snorts. "I remember you. And your brother. Where's your brother now?"

One time, not the last time my brother was here but before that, Big Eddie took me to the park on the south end of Lake Madeline. When we got to the playground, the three Schmidt kids were already on the equipment. Alyssa was on the swings, and her brothers, who were about eight and ten at the time, were jumping off the monkey bars. The park has a big slide and ramp structure that looks like a pirate ship. Big Eddie stood at the bottom of the slide and watched me climb up. When I got to the top, I looked down. I was only six, maybe seven, so I thought it was super high. I stopped, and when I did, one of the Schmidt boys shoved me into the railing of the slide's landing.

"Where are you and your dumb brother from anyhow?" Ivan asks me now. He has pimples on his forehead, and his shirt is so threadbare, I can practically see his belly button.

"Me? Here," I say. "Minneapolis."

"No, where are you *from*?" He says "from" slowly like I don't speak English.

I squint at him. Every time I meet new kids, a new family, new teachers, they always ask, *Where are you from?* The *from* they're asking about, the answer they want, is a place, a country, a continent. Maybe it's my last name, maybe it's my dark hair, but people always think I'm from somewhere else. Anywhere but Minnesota.

So sometimes I say South America. Sometimes I say Timbuktu. Sometimes I say Mars.

"Mars," I say to Alyssa's brothers. Not that it's a good idea. I should be keeping my mouth shut.

Alyssa laughs, but not like it's funny.

"Well, you look like a spic to me," Mason says.

"Yeah, those spics love catching polluted fish on the lake." Ivan scoots his bike closer to me. I can't back up because I'm all the way in the corner of the T of the dock.

"He's from Mexico," Alyssa volunteers. "Or maybe Colombia?" I regret the country report I did last year for Hispanic Heritage Month.

Our teacher, Ms. Hanover, had explained that "Hispanic" meant "people from Latin American or South American backgrounds." There was the astronaut Ellen Ochoa. There was some teacher from long ago named Jaime Escalante. Roberto Clemente was a baseball player that a couple of baseball fans in the class had heard of. But the assignment didn't have anything to do with people. The assignment was to choose a Latin American country to research. Liam and I were partners, and we chose Colombia. Alyssa and Emma Matthews did Costa Rica.

"Shut up, Alyssa," says Ivan, who is off his bike now.

"You got some cocaine for us?" says Mason. He leans his bicycle against his brother's, and both bikes topple over. The movement on the dock makes little waves on the water, sending ripples across . . . to where? What if the ripples could be felt by the toddlers swimming at the beach at the other end of the lake?

"You must love drinkin' coffee," Mason says in some weird sort of accent that I can only assume is supposed to be Spanish but sounds nothing like the way Big Eddie does when he speaks. Mason steps over the fallen bikes and gets near enough to poke me in the stomach, where the life jacket puffs out. "Eh, Juan Valdez?"

"Leave me alone," I say, trying to back up again but getting stopped by the railing. The two Schmidt kids inch closer. If Big Eddie were here, he'd stop them like he did when I was little.

After Mason Schmidt shoved me that day on the slide, Big Eddie shouted, "What do you think you're doing, shrimp?"

Mason turned at the sound of my brother's voice. "What are you gonna do about it, spic?" Mason said, his voice pointed and mean.

"You better leave him alone, cabrón." Just as Big Eddie said what I was pretty sure was a bad word, Mason pushed me again, this time so hard that I tumbled down the slide. Big Eddie ran to catch me, but he was too late. My nose went deep into the wood shavings, and I could taste blood. I started to cry. When Mason came down the slide laughing, Big Eddie was already there. He was fourteen and big enough to scoop me up in one arm and grab hold of Mason's T-shirt with the other, right at the neck. "Don't you touch him again, *little* boy."

Now, as the Schmidt brothers inch closer to me, it's clear that Big Eddie didn't fix anything.

"Look," Ivan says, grabbing the rod, "we found a fishing pole. I've always wanted a fishing pole."

And then, as if I have no control over what comes out of my mouth, I say, "It's called a fishing rod, idiots."

Alyssa's two brothers lunge at me and grab both my arms and shove me, hard. I stumble back against the railing. One of them yanks my arm behind my back, and the other one snatches Papa's fishing rod.

"Give it," I say, twisting out of Ivan's hold.

"Are you going to cry?" Mason throws the rod like a javelin. What if it sinks? What if I lose Papa's rod? How will I fish? How will I win the tournament and get a medal just like his and get the money to help Mama? It feels like my whole life depends on that fishing rod, which is now flying through the air.

I dive for the rod but notice a split second too late that my shoelace is untied. And like a cartoon character, I sprawl across the dock. But I'm not hurt, thanks to the cushioning effect of the life jacket. And luckily for me, Mason is no athlete. The end of the rod skids into the water, its reel caught on the dock.

A shadow falls over us. "What's the trouble here?" A tall man with dreadlocks is on the dock, his dirty bucket in one hand and rod in the other. "No bikes allowed on the dock."

Alyssa has already ridden to shore by the time her brothers are back on their bikes.

"Spic," they spit at me with venom that I can almost taste. I kneel on the dock and reach for my rod. Other than being wet, it's not in any worse shape than it was before.

"Thanks," I say to the fisherman, but he has already turned back to his bucket.

I breathe. My chest feels like I ran a mile. I'm going to show them, show everyone. I look into the water. I'm going to catch the biggest fish ever. I'm going to win that tournament.

6

WHEN I GET HOME from the dock, Mama's on the phone. She pulls it away from her ear as I walk in. "Do you want to talk to Liam?"

I nod. Maybe I'll tell him about the Schmidt kids. Jerks.

"Sarah," Mama says into the phone, "here's Little Eddie."

I shake my head at Mama for calling me Little Eddie. It's so embarrassing when she does it in front of other people. "Hey," I say, taking the phone.

"Hi, Eddie!" I can hear the exclamation mark in Liam's voice. I open my mouth to speak, but Liam is off. Without taking a breath, he tells me about his new neighborhood and the community center and the stepbrothers. *"We're all coming back to Minnesota maybe for Christmas!"* More exclamation marks. *"It's hecka cool!"*

"Cool," I say. I want to ask him about the word "spic." I

want to tell him about escaping those bullies. But Liam just goes on about how there's no day camp in Brooklyn, just the community center, and Enrique to take him places. Then I hear a crash and Clara's familiar little giggle alongside the laughter of people I can't identify. Liam, who used to sleep over at the old apartment and hang out after school and catch frogs in the parking lot, is doing all those things—or different things, I guess—far away. Now it's just me. I don't feel like I belong anywhere anymore.

Between giggles, Liam says, *"I gotta go."* There's another crash in the background. *"Bye!"*

Even though I can hear Mama making dinner in the kitchen, the duplex echoes, reminding me how lonely it is here. It's not fair. Thinking of Liam so far away and having his own, new life makes me so angry that I decide I'm not going to say good-bye back. But it doesn't matter because Liam hangs up so fast, I don't get a chance.

I drop Mama's phone onto the coffee table and go into my room, slamming the door behind me. In the S-T volume of my encyclopedia, I look for the word "spic," but it's not in there. I pick up another volume and scan the entry for fishing. It's fifteen pages long and has lots of pictures. It says: *Although fishing is now considered a sport, it was originally a means of getting food to eat. Evidence dating back to 2000 BC shows that ancient humans caught fish with nets and rods.*

I bet ancient humans didn't wear life jackets. I go into the garage and stuff the life vest between two cardboard boxes on one of the shelves. I never want to see it again. I lean the rod against the back corner with the other one and check the side door that opens into the alley. It's an old wooden door with a glass window that rattles when you slam the door shut. And you have to really slam it because it sticks. I make sure the door is latched and locked—not that anyone would want to steal any of the junk in here.

While she's cooking dinner, Mama goes on about Big Eddie's arrival on Monday, like when we'll pick him up at the airport and what else we need to do to get ready. With one hand she stirs the vegetarian goop she calls ragout, and with the other she writes a list.

"I bought him a bus pass. Did I get sheets?"

"Last week," I remind her.

"Right. Can you help me move the desk into his room?"

I don't remind her that it's more of a table than a desk. It's hard to imagine Big Eddie doing homework at it. He usually just visits for a couple of weeks, and I'm so glad he's actually going to be here all summer. Even if he does have to take classes at the university.

"Don't let me forget to hang the blinds. And get a new pillow." She writes on her list and then sets it aside. "Hopefully that's it." She ladles ragout and rice onto two plates and sits down.

"Can you buy me bait?" I ask.

She scrunches her nose. "You mean worms?" She shakes her head. "That's what a big brother is for, Little Eddie." I guess both of us can't wait for Big Eddie to get here.

We take turns sprinkling salt onto our food. Sometimes

Mama is a good cook, and sometimes she's not.

"Did you know you can use salt to get leeches off?" I ask. I read that in my encyclopedia. "It kills them."

"Yuck." Mama shakes her head.

I watch her take a sip of water, and then I ask her what "spic" means.

Her lips press together. "Did you hear that at camp?" I shake my head. "Then where?" She sets down the forkful of zucchini that was headed for her mouth. I personally hate zucchini. It's always trying to trick you into thinking it's cucumber. I hate when one thing is like another only not. Like sugar-free gum or soccer in gym class or animated movies that teach about the human body.

"Nowhere," I lie. If I tell her about what happened with Alyssa's brothers, she'll never let me go to the dock again—even *with* a life vest. And I'll never learn to fish, and I'll never catch the big one, and I'll never win the tournament. And I'll never get to be like Papa.

"Eat your vegetables," Mama says. She chews. A chickadee calls outside the kitchen window and the refrigerator hums. "'Spic' is a term that doesn't really mean anything. Do you know what the N-word is?"

I nod slowly. I know exactly which word she's talking about. Worse than all the other curse words. Worse than the S-word, worse than the F-word. There might be some others, but I'm not sure. Mama doesn't like cursing.

"They're words meant to hurt you. Name-calling. Do you remember when you called Liam a poophead?"

"I was only six!" I protest. "And he called me a butthead."

"Well," she says, "then you know that everyone gets called names sometimes."

"Did Papa get called names?"

Mama is quiet. She pretends to be fascinated by a bird on the feeder outside, but maybe she's deciding whether this is something she wants to tell me. Sometimes it seems like she thinks if she tells me stuff about Papa, her memories will run out, get used up like the bottles of coolant she has to add to her car.

"Even Papa," she says finally. "When your father was your age, he was teased for being smart. Lambón. Teacher's pet, brownnoser. You know—those kinds of names. There was a bully, he told me, who used to follow him home from school every day and throw rocks at him. He even had a scar." Mama puts down her fork and rubs my back, just under my left shoulder blade. "Right here. But one day there was a radio announcement for an essay contest. The prize was money—I don't remember how much—and the winner also got to read his essay on the radio."

I listen and hold on to this story of Papa, one of the few she's told me over the last seven years. It's like a birthday present to hear it.

"Did Papa win?"

Mama shakes her head and smiles. "Not quite. What happened, he told me, was that the bully was one of those show-offs and wanted to be on the radio. He and your papa made a deal: Eduardo would write the essay, and the bully would stop throwing rocks."

"That's not fair," I humph.

"I don't know if Papa thought it was fair or not, but he wrote the essay and it actually won the contest, so he was proud of that. And, anyway, he was pretty shy, so he wouldn't have wanted to be on the radio. After that, the bully stopped throwing rocks even though he still called your papa names. But the names became just words. They didn't hurt anymore."

"But 'spic'?" I ask.

Mama strokes my back in the place where Papa had a scar I never knew about. "Even that name is just a word. Some people use certain words to make people that are different from them feel bad." She's raising her voice now, not smiling. She's not angry—or, at least, not angry at me. "But words are just words."

"What does it mean?" I push the zucchini around on my plate, hoping that she'll forget to make me eat it.

"It's a jumble of letters taken from the word 'Hispanic.' You know. Latino. Latinx."

"Was Papa Latino?"

"He was Colombian, so yes."

"What about Big Eddie?"

"Him, too. And also you, Little Eddie."

I think of the Hispanic Heritage Month projects. I don't feel Hispanic or Latino. Liam didn't think I counted as Colombian. I don't feel like Big Eddie or Papa. I look over at the kitchen window, but there are no birds on the feeder now. I don't know who I am.

"Be careful of anyone who uses that word. Any of those words—"

The phone interrupts her. She grins wide when she looks

at the number. "It's your brother," she says. "Mijo," Mama answers with a smile, and I smile too, even though it's kind of annoying when she speaks Spanish to Big Eddie and not me. But then her smile fades, and she seems to shrink a little.

"What is it?" I ask, tugging at her sleeve. She bats my hand away and keeps listening, murmuring yes and no. I watch her like I watched the fish in the water at the lake, keeping my eye on her so I don't miss anything.

At last she looks at me and says, "Little Eddie." Her voice is thin and strange. "I'm sorry, but . . . Big Eddie's not coming."

7

AT FIRST MAMA is upset at Big Eddie for not telling us sooner that his abuela has cancer. But then it turns out that he just found out. His grandmother had been keeping her illness a secret.

"She's been kind of weak," he says. He's on speaker, and Mama nods at the phone even though Big Eddie can't see that.

"How long has she been sick?" she asks.

"I don't know. She won't tell me. She doesn't want chemotherapy." Big Eddie's voice gets a snag in it like when a zipper catches on a sleeping bag. *"She doesn't want anything."*

"Oh, I'm so sorry about your abuela," Mama says. She offers to do whatever she can. Then she starts asking nurse-type questions about the medication and the blood pressure and the oxygen levels. She asks so many questions, I quit listening.

I know that "abuela" means "grandmother." But I don't have one of those. Or a grandfather. Well, I suppose everyone does, technically. My grandparents would be the parents of Mama and Papa. But Papa's parents died long before I was born. And last we heard, Mama's parents lived in southern Florida, but they don't speak to their only daughter. They didn't like her Colombian husband. My dad. Long ago, even though they lived in Florida, where it's hot, they used to send Christmas cards with winter scenes. Mama still has the cards saved in the box of Christmas decorations, and the glitter from the fake snow gets all over everything. But now nothing arrives. No cards, no birthday money, not even a condolence card after Eduardo Aguado León died. I know all this because Mama tells this story about her mom and dad—the people who should be my grandparents—in a sort of singsong voice, a practiced story. I wonder if I tell the story of not having a dad in a practiced, singsong voice.

I hear my name. *"You still there, Little Eddie?"*

"I'm here," I answer.

"I'm sorry I have to cancel my trip."

"Yeah," I say quietly. "What about summer school? What about college?"

"I'll still go, just later. Abuela wants me to go, but I'll defer for now. Maybe until September," he says, brushing away my question like he's batting at mosquitoes.

46

"Don't worry about that, mijo. I'll call the university tomorrow," Mama says to Big Eddie.

"Right now, what Abuela would really like is for you to come here. Please come to Cartagena. She wants to see you."

My heart leaps. Colombia? Me in Colombia?

"Abuela would like to invite you both." Big Eddie sounds formal, like this is an invitation on thick paper in gold ink.

"It's impossible." Mama sounds sad.

"It would mean so much to Abuela to meet Little Eddie."

"Even if we could afford the flight, I can't leave work. I started a new job—my first nursing job—and there's no way I can get time off. And even if I could, the flight . . ." Mama trails off. She must be trying to figure out how it might work, but she's also thinking about the rent on the duplex and the nursing school loans and the car with the strange smell. If only the Fourteenth Annual Arne Hopkins Dock Fishing Tournament were tomorrow. I would win it and use the prize money to buy our way to Colombia. To Big Eddie. To the abuela I've never met.

"We can exchange the plane ticket. One Eddie for another." My half brother's voice is quiet but firm. *"Send Little Eddie."*

The sentence that Big Eddie lets travel through the phone, across the continents, over the distance, is so small and yet so big. *Send Little Eddie.* Something shifts in the room, and I can feel Mama sigh.

Me.

In Colombia.

By myself.

· ✳ · ✳ ·

Later, after I've scraped the uneaten zucchini into the trash and helped Mama wash dishes, I'm watching TV as if nothing has changed, but I'm holding my breath in case it really might be happening.

Mama sits next to me on the couch. "Do you want to go?"

"When would I go?" The tournament is in five and a half weeks. I need to be back by then. Because I need to win a medal like Papa's. Don't I?

"Soon," she says. "Abuela is very sick."

I've never been on a plane, much less to another country. And what do I know of Colombia? I know that Colombia is famous for illegal things like cocaine and other drugs, and for legal things like coffee. Thanks to my country report, I also know that Colombia is the only South American country to touch both the Atlantic and the Pacific Oceans, that the capital city of Bogotá is more than a mile and a half above sea level, and that the condor is the national bird. When Liam and I handed in our Colombia report to Ms. Hanover, all she did was glance at the poster and say, "You spelled it wrong." We looked at Liam's artwork (pretty nice, if you ask me) of coffee plantations and a hand-drawn map. There were large bubble letters (a little crooked) that I had drawn, spelling out the country's name. "You spelled 'Colombia' wrong," my teacher said again.

"But that's how it's spelled." I pointed at the letters.

"He should know," Liam said. "His dad is from there."

"I'm sorry, Eddie, but it has a *U*, not another *O*." Ms. Hanover later deducted five points for the spelling.

"Why me?" I ask Mama now. "Why does Abuela want me to visit her? She doesn't even know me."

"She loved your father very much. He lived with Abuela and Big Eddie after his first wife—Big Eddie's mom—died and before he went to graduate school here." I hold my whole body still, listening with all my strength to Mama's story about Papa. This is one of her memories she's letting me have. "After we got married," Mama says, "we went to Colombia for a while and lived with Ana María—that's Abuela's name—for six months."

Somewhere in the back of my mind, I knew that Mama and Papa lived in Colombia. But it's hard to imagine. *My mom? In South America?*

"Is that where you learned Spanish?"

She nods. "I'm sorry I didn't teach you." She smooths down my hair. Her sadness seems especially thick tonight. It's more like a dense fog than the usual light mist. I run my fingers through my hair, trying to keep the sadness from landing on me too.

On Friday the Kamp Kids counselors bring us to the lake and hand out Popsicles. This time Cameron and I aren't the only campers on the dock. A group of younger kids has followed us. I guess those kids think it's pretty cool to follow a black-haired boy and a purple-haired girl.

"Last day, right?" Cameron says, biting off the end of her lime Popsicle. "No more Kamp Kids now that your brother's coming?"

"Um." I lick my Popsicle. "Except—my brother's not coming."

"What? Why?"

"His grandma's sick."

"That's not fair." She takes another bite of her Popsicle with her bunny teeth. Then she smiles with green lips. "But that means you'll be back at Kamp Kids next week? Maybe tomorrow we can meet to practice our fishing. Now that we have your dad's gear."

"I can't."

"But we have to practice. We already sent in the entry form—and the money!" Cameron leans down and looks me in the eye. The purple ends of her hair tickle my nose. "Mr. Eddie, we have a tournament to win."

I bat her away. "No, I really can't. Because . . . well, I'm going to Colombia."

Ever since Big Eddie told us about his abuela, Mama has been making phone calls and going to the library, where she's been sending faxes to the Colombian consulate so that Big Eddie can change his plans. The university is letting him start the international student program in the fall instead of now, but he didn't really seem to care about all that.

Mama also dug out my passport that's never been used. Once, a few years after Papa died, she was going to take me to Colombia, but it never happened. She says we're lucky that my passport isn't expired yet. Getting the right paperwork for me to travel out of the country by myself hasn't been as easy. Mama had to write a letter and take it to a notary. In the N-O-P volume of my encyclopedia, I learned that a notary is basically someone whose job is to make sure people don't cheat. That sounds like a useful person to have around.

Cameron turns to watch the little kids screaming as one of their Popsicle sticks falls into the water. Then they all drop theirs in on purpose and scream some more.

"Colombia," Cameron says with her back to me. "Fancy." She doesn't say it like she thinks it's fancy. Then I remember how she wants to visit her mom in California. "How many times have you been there?" she asks.

"Never."

"You and your mom are going?"

"No, just me. Since my brother's not coming, we used his refund to buy my ticket. But my mom can't go because she just started her job at the hospital. No vacation time."

Cameron rolls her eyes. "My dad never takes any time off. Ever."

A swarm of fish is clumped around the floating Popsicle sticks. The fish. That I'm going to catch. But not right now.

"I guess that means you'll be an unaccompanied minor?"

"Yep," I say. Mama had to pay extra for my ticket since I'll be traveling by myself.

"I've done it."

"What's it like?" I ask—not that I'm worried.

"You get a flight attendant to take care of you when you aren't with your mom or dad. You get a sticker or button. Sometimes they give you extra snacks and blankets. Maybe you'll get a really hot lady and you'll fall in love and stay on the plane forever and ever."

I laugh, but my stomach feels like the Popsicle sticks are jabbing into it. Am I ready to go to another country by myself? Am I ready to leave Mama and Cameron and Lake Mad and all those fish? Am I ready to see my brother in Cartagena?

Cameron squints at me and says, "Nah. I bet you get a crusty old man that smells like pee."

That would be just my luck.

8

I CLOSE MY EYES and submerge my head, careful not to let any waves splash over the sides of the bathtub. Through the water, I can hear Mama calling me. Is this what it sounds like if you're a fish, all the sounds garbled together?

I resurface and hear Mama ask, "Are you done in there?" She's just outside the bathroom door.

"Almost." I pull out the rubber stopper in the tub. The water makes a satisfying sucking noise. In the old apartment, the shower stall drain never did that.

"We've got to get you to the airport soon."

I lurch out and grab a towel just in case she decides to barge in. "Okay!"

"Twenty-five minutes, Little Eddie."

I pull on my jeans and yank on a T-shirt. There's so much

Anika Fajardo

I still have to do: find a place in my suitcase for all the pres-
ents Mama has suddenly decided I need to take, fit the C
volume of my encyclopedia into my backpack, find my flip-
flops that I said were not lost, and scrape the goose poop
from my left sneaker. And then I'll be on a plane. I wipe the
steam off the mirror and comb my hair out of my face. First
flight, first time out of the country. Twenty-five minutes
sounds as short as a blip and also as long as the month I'll
be in Colombia.

After much badgering from Mama, we're finally out of
the house with my backpack on my back, my flip-flops
found and in my suitcase, and my sneakers clean. When
we arrive at the airport, Mama does her fast walk across the
parking ramp. She's already at the glass doors of the elevator
vestibule by the time I catch up. You would think she's the
one catching a flight.

We rushed to get to the airport, yet now that we're here,
we have to wait. First we wait for the ticketing agent to
sign me in as an unaccompanied minor. They check all
the paperwork Mama gives them and then they give me a
sticker to wear, just like Cameron said they would. It has
wings as if I'm the one who's going to do the flying. Then
we wait for Mama to get a special pass so she can come with
me to the gate. My suitcase gets weighed and sent by itself
on a little conveyor belt. She buys me a bottle of water and
a packet of red licorice to take on the plane.

After we get through the long security lines, Mama
waits with me in the low-ceilinged departure gate filled
with other sons and brothers, aunties and cousins, leaving

54

for Miami. I know that not all of them are continuing on
to Colombia, since I have to change planes before I get to
Cartagena, but I look around to try to guess who might
be. Maybe the grandma and grandpa with three teenage
girls speaking Spanish? Maybe the man in a white hat and
wearing a goatee? Maybe the guy with blond curly hair
and a huge dirty backpack? Who knows? The only one I
know for sure is me.

"Are you positive you have everything?" Mama asks, and
then she uses her thumb to wipe something away from my
cheek. She reaches into the outside pocket of my backpack
and checks for the ticket. I look it over. Minneapolis, Minnesota, to Cartagena, Colombia. Two *O*s.

Mama now rummages around in her big purse. She pulls
out a phone—her old cell phone—and hands it to me.

"For me?" I'm the only kid in the whole world who
doesn't have a phone. I click on the camera and, before she
can say anything, I snap a picture of her.

"This is for me to know you're safe," she says, taking it
out of my hand. "Big Eddie helped set up the calling plan."
She opens the call feature and hands it back. "See? I put in
our numbers. Me and Big Eddie."

"Thank you!" I wrap my arms around her neck.

"Here's the charger," she says, digging into her bag again.

I open my backpack and take a folded-up piece of paper
out of the inside pocket. Cameron's phone number is written in orange crayon. She gave it to me on my last day
of camp. I type it into my new phone. Now I have three
contacts.

"Do you want Liam's number?" Mama enters it into my phone without waiting for an answer.

Four contacts.

I switch to the app store. "Can I play games on the plane? What apps does it have?"

"It's *only* for calling me and, when you have Wi-Fi, texting," Mama says in her you're-going-to-get-in-trouble-if-you-don't-listen voice. "It's not going to work very well since it's old, and in Colombia you'll need to find Wi-Fi if you want to use the internet. Your brother says that texting will be the cheapest."

Sometimes Mama really knows how to get a guy down. But I nod. At least I have a phone.

"Can I text my friends right now?"

Mama nods, but doesn't look away. So while she's watching me, I type a message to one of the four contacts in my phone:

Hi, Liam! I got a phone and I'm going to Colombia!

I add a miniature red, blue, and yellow Colombian flag emoji and hit send. He doesn't answer right away. Then I remember that he might not recognize my new phone, so I send another message:

P.S. This is Eddie.

Then I text Cameron:

I got a phone! I'm at the airport about to leave for Colombia.

I add a tongue-sticking-out face and hit send.

I look up and see that Mama's eyes are filled with tears. They wait like the planes lined up outside on the runway.

I have to look away before they take off. "Promise to text me," she says. "I'm going to miss you."

"I promise," I tell Mama, and hug her tight. This time it feels like she's the one who's going to float away.

Last year my teacher gave us a bonus spelling word. "Discombobulate: to upset or confuse." We thought it was a funny word. Now I'm glad I learned it, because it perfectly describes how I feel right now. Cameron sure was right when she said life is something. One moment you're standing on a fishing dock in Minnesota, and the next you're in a foreign country all by yourself.

I'm waiting for my luggage with the flight attendant/babysitter at the Cartagena airport. I haven't seen my suitcase since Minneapolis, even though I got off one plane and onto another in Miami, followed the whole time by my babysitter. In one hand I grip Papa's medal. In the other, I hold my new phone like it's a life vest. The airport has Wi-Fi, so I connect and type a new message.

Flight attendant was not hot. Did not smell like pee.

I add a smiley face. Then I worry Cameron won't get it. Then I worry that I sound dumb. I look around the baggage claim area and worry that I won't recognize my brother, who is coming to meet me as soon as I get my luggage. I watch the suitcases pour out of the carousel, piling against each other, knocking into one another. Sometimes my worries feel like that, all of them piling up. What if Big Eddie doesn't show? What if I never get home to Minnesota? What if I don't catch a fish?

My suitcase on wheels is now inching its way along the carousel. "Is this yours, Edward?" the flight attendant asks. She pulls it off and sets it upright next to me just as I hear a familiar voice.

"Little Eddie!"

And then I'm standing in front of a man who hardly looks like a teenager anymore. It's been three years, and now my brother, at nineteen, is practically an adult. He's wearing slim-fitting jeans and a long-sleeve shirt. He hugs me and smiles, but his eyes are sad. Sad like Mama's are sometimes.

"Hermanito," Big Eddie says, hugging me, messing up my hair. "My little brother."

He scoops up my suitcase, shows his ID to the flight attendant, signs a paper, and that's the end of the babysitter.

I follow my brother to the airport's exit. A swarm of black-haired people, their skin yellowed in the harsh lighting, look at me without really seeing me. The automatic doors open and shut with a swooshing sound like someone diving into a lake.

I would love to jump into Lake Mad right now. Even the humidity of Minnesota summers hasn't prepared me for this wall of heat. I thought inside the airport was hot, but the heat outside feels like an evil villain wanting to eat me alive.

"I'm so glad you're here," Big Eddie says as we walk through the dark parking lot. I can't believe he's wearing pants and long sleeves. "And Abuela is too." He heaves my suitcase into the trunk of a tiny blue car. I smile awkwardly.

Talking to him in person is different from talking to him on the phone. I was eight the last time I saw him. And now. Now he's like a stranger. Only not.

"¿Listo?" Big Eddie turns the ignition, and the car jerks to life, along with a booming bass rhythm. Big Eddie switches off the radio.

"It's hot," I say. "Can we have the air-conditioning?"

"In this old car?" He laughs and then opens the windows. The breeze doesn't cool me down. "Are you hungry? We're going straight home," he explains in English even more accented than I remember. "We can eat there."

As he careens around corners, he shouts, "Hold on!" and he laughs his familiar laugh when I shriek at the turns. He loves to drive. When he visited three years ago, he was sixteen and was always asking to drive Mama's car. She told him he needed an international driver's license, because she's a rule-follower like that. She let him drive once, but he went so fast on the little side streets, she said she almost had a seizure.

Now I see what she meant. He weaves in and out of traffic. Motorbikes whiz past. We lurch to a stop at an intersection where women with bags slung over their shoulders offer to sell candies and strange fruit. He takes off once the intersection is clear, zooming around corners. Even though it's dark out, the city of Cartagena is alive, pulsing. I've never seen so many people out at night except for when Mama and I go see fireworks on the Fourth of July.

Big Eddie pulls the car to a stop at another red light. A man stands in the spotlight of the cars' headlights and starts to juggle knives—actual knives. Music pours out of a shop-front that smells like burgers, only different.

"Hermanito," Big Eddie says, shifting the car into gear when the light turns green and the juggler steps aside to let the traffic pass. "What do you think of my country?"

"Um," I say, not really listening. I feel jumbled and shaken, and not just because of Big Eddie's driving. This isn't anything like the pictures of Colombia in the C volume of my encyclopedia that I read on the plane.

Big Eddie socks my shoulder. "This is tu patria, Little Eddie. Your homeland."

My homeland? I silently shape my mouth into the Spanish word: pah-tree-ah. It feels strange, but maybe strange is okay.

I hear a pinging noise. It's coming from my pocket. I pull out my phone as Big Eddie swings the car around a corner. I didn't think my phone would work, but there is a text from Cameron.

Hey, you fisherman. Sorry your flight attendant wasn't hot. My dad is talking about getting me a fishing rod, but he always promises and never delivers. I went to the dock and dropped a yogurt in. Lots of fish came up to eat it. But no sign of the big one. Stay cool.

I smile. She's as wacky as her purple hair.

Another ping. Mama.

Did you arrive in one piece? Please message me so I don't worry. I checked the weather, and it says it's supposed to be 98 degrees in Cartagena. Don't forget sunscreen. And drink plenty of water. Love you!

There's a funny twinge at the back of my throat at the thought of Mama worrying about me. I answer her.

I'm here with Big Eddie. He's super tall!

Mama pings me again.

P.S. Drink only bottled water!!!

I send a thumbs-up to Mama, and she immediately texts back with three pink hearts.

"Wow, Little Eddie," my brother says as he pulls the car into a driveway between two small, low houses. "You're a popular kid. Is that your girlfriend?"

I'm glad it's dark so that he can't see me turn red. I bet he never turns red. He probably never gets embarrassed.

"It's just my mom." I don't tell him about Cameron.

"Did you tell Liz you got here safe? She's going to worry otherwise. We had to convince her that we would take care of you and that you wouldn't be in the way." He turns off the car, and in the sudden quiet, I hear the distant laughter of children. "Ya llegamos. We're here."

While Big Eddie gets my suitcase from the trunk, I look at the text from Cameron again. I don't know what to say to her, so I take a picture of Big Eddie bringing my luggage through a small gate to the house. He turns when the flash goes off, and his face is strangely lit like he's a ghost. I send her the picture anyway. She sends back a smiley face, and my own face becomes smiley too.

9

"¿CÓMO AMANECISTE?" a voice asks. In the yellow morning light, I see a man with black hair leaning over me. Across the small room is an unmade bed that matches the one I'm lying in. Both beds have dark wood headboards and footboards. Between them is a matching nightstand with a lamp crowded next to a pile of magazines. The walls are hidden by posters of shiny cars and of singers I don't recognize. The bedroom is as messy as Liam's. A bookshelf is crammed with stuff: a trophy in the shape of a soccer player, a white seashell the size of my head, a stuffed monkey with one eye missing, and a stack of postcards. I feel clammy and thirsty, like I've been in a desert for forty days (not that I've ever seen a desert).

"How did you sleep?" asks the man.

Oh.

That's not a man. It's Big Eddie. I untangle myself from the damp sheets.

Last night Abuela's house was a blur of white tile floors and dark wood furniture. Abuela was at the hospital, so Big Eddie made me a ham and cheese sandwich in a little sandwich press. He gave me a glass bottle of Coca-Cola even though it has caffeine and it was after nine. At bedtime he showed me how he lines up six empty beer bottles across the floor tiles in front of the door. "In case someone gets through the locks," he told me, "the noise will wake me up, and *bam*—" Big Eddie made a slicing motion with his hand, and I laughed.

"My grandmother can leave the hospital this morning," Big Eddie says now. "I'm going to bring her home."

I still feel discombobulated. I rub my eyes again. Maybe this is what a fish feels like when it's pulled out of the water.

"I'm leaving now, but Nita, Abuela's maid, is here."

A maid? "Is Abuela rich?"

"Rich? No. Why?" Big Eddie looks confused. "Oh, the maid. Lots of families have maids here. People need work. Nita doesn't speak any English, but you'll be fine. She can make you breakfast."

After he leaves, I climb out of bed, my feet hitting the tiles. When I jerk from the startling cold of the floor, my arm hits the nightstand, and all the magazines slide to the floor. Stacking them back into a pile, I examine each one. Maybe I can learn something about my half brother by studying his stuff.

The magazines are all in Spanish. They have different

titles, but each one has a car and a woman on the cover. All the women are smiling and wearing very little clothing, and they're draped across the hoods of the cars in what look like very uncomfortable positions. In fact, I get a little uncomfortable just looking at them.

Ping. I pull my phone out of the pocket of my jeans that are on the floor in a heap. The text is from Cameron.

Liam hasn't answered yet.

Cameron's message contains a blurry photo and the word "Duckling." I zoom in and count six baby ducks swimming in a crooked line.

In the early summer, the mallard ducks parade their fuzzy ducklings around Lake Mad like the human moms with their strollers. Back home I read about ducks in the D-E-F volume of my encyclopedia. Mallards, like chickadees, are native to North America. I type a reply:

Did you know that mallard ducks don't live in Colombia? I wonder if I should. Happy fishing.

I pull on a pair of shorts from my suitcase, slip Papa's medal into the pocket, and go into the hallway. The entire house has the same white tiles. I've never seen a house with floors like this. Our old apartment had worn wood floors, and our new duplex has carpeting.

Ping. I read Cameron's message.

Haven't fished yet. Still no rod. Don't stay there forever! I need a partner!

I smile. Even though I just met her, she already seems like more of a friend than Liam. Why hasn't he texted me back yet? I stuff the phone into my pocket, ready to explore. To my left is a heavy wooden door with a lattice of black bars covering its rectangular window. Beyond the window, I can hear the rumble of cars in the street out front. Through the bars, I see a small yard surrounded by a fence, and a walkway splitting it neatly in half. Across the hall, a door is partway open. I peek in. The curtains are green and match the bedspread. An arrangement of black-and-white photos in gold frames clutters the bedside table, which is crowded with medicine bottles. A stale smell seeps out. It must be Abuela's room. I wrinkle my nose. It's the tangy, sour scent that infects Mama's work clothes and reminds me of the mustiness of Papa's hospital room. I've been trying not to think too much about Big Eddie's grandmother being sick, even though that's why I'm here.

At the end of the hallway is a living room, dining room, and kitchen that all open onto what looks to me like an indoor backyard. Brick walls, as tall as the one-story house, enclose a cement patio, a patch of green grass, and a few shrubs. A bright green tree in the courtyard's center reaches for the scorching sun above. In the kitchen, a short, round woman in jeans and a T-shirt that says "pretty" in sparkly letters is mopping the floor. Is this the maid? She doesn't look like a maid. Not like a maid in a movie, not anything like Cinderella.

She sees me and smiles. She points at herself. "Nita," she says, and then says about a hundred other words in Spanish.

I stare at her. I can't help it. What am I supposed to say?

She leans her mop against the wall and lifts two brown eggs from a tray on the counter. Oh, she wants to cook me breakfast. But my stomach feels funny. And I've never seen eggs not from a refrigerator. I shake my head.

She puts down the eggs and grabs a pitcher. Her eyebrows go up. I come closer and see that it's some kind of juice. I nod. "Okay," I say. And then I say, "Vale," the way Big Eddie taught me. That makes her go wild with excitement. I feel like a baby saying his first word.

She pours juice for me and says something else in Spanish. I don't know what kind of juice this is—it tastes supersweet at first, but after I swallow, a shock of sour. And with that sip, it hits me that I am in Colombia. South America. Somewhere out there is the Caribbean Sea. During the flight I read in my encyclopedia that the water of the Caribbean is famous for being clear, blue, and warm. And filled with fish. I hope Big Eddie will take me fishing, even though his grandmother is sick. Maybe he'll want a break. And I need to practice. If I can catch a fish in the Caribbean, catching one in an old Minnesota lake will be easy.

I walk into the courtyard. The tree in the middle of the patio is not very tall but has a twisted trunk. One branch is held up by two pieces of wood nailed together. Big yellowish-green spheres hang from the tree branches. Limes? I look closer. No, they have little nubs like lemons. It's funny because I know that lemons come from trees the way I know milk comes from cows, but it's different to see it for myself. If you don't see where something came from, it's hard to believe it actually did.

After setting my juice glass down on the patio bricks, I grab a yellow fruit from a low branch. I yank until it drops into my hand. The lemon is warm, almost as warm as the air. I toss the fruit up and catch it again. Toss. Catch. It feels like I'm inside a secret garden. A steaming hot secret Colombian garden. From over the courtyard's brick walls, I can hear the drone of a television from some other house, and in the opposite direction the chatter of what sounds like very loud and wild children.

Toss. Catch. The lemon's citrus smell fills the air. Maybe catching a fish is as easy as this. I hear Nita chopping something in the kitchen. The rhythm is like a drumbeat. Toss. Catch.

I'm just about to toss the lemon one more time, when something comes soaring over the courtyard's wall. A soccer ball, black and white with frayed stitching. Above me, the top slats of a wooden ladder appear, followed by a small brown face. The face says something to me in Spanish. I mean, I knew everyone here would speak Spanish, but it still surprises me to hear words I don't understand coming out of a little kid.

"I don't speak Spanish," I call up to the boy. He's about seven or eight. The boy laughs and talks to whoever is on his side of the wall. I hear more laughter, and more brown faces appear.

"Hola," I say, and wave to the two—no, three—faces. They burst into giggles. I feel like a goldfish in a bowl.

"Soo-kur," the first boy says. "Fútbol." He points at the ball again.

I set my lemon on the patio next to my empty juice glass and grab the ball from under the branches of the tree. I line the ball up for the kick. In third and fourth grades, I played on the park soccer league, midfield. I wasn't that good, but I could keep away opponents with some quick dribbling and sometimes a pass (even if it was usually accidental). During one of the last games of my last season, my team was losing by eight points. The other team had a girl center with a wicked kick. You should've seen the parents. Shouting, jumping on the sidelines. "Don't let her through!" they called. "Watch the open spots!"

We lost. Like I said, the girl was wicked good. After we all high-fived, I found Mama in her lawn chair, with her usual book open in her lap. She didn't always pay attention, but she always came to my games.

"Great game," she said, looking at me from behind large sunglasses.

"What do you mean 'great game'?" said a dad behind her. His son was the forward on my team. The dad and son sometimes gave me rides to practice when Mama was at nursing school. "Eddie could have hustled," the dad said, loud enough for everyone to hear. "I thought Colombians could play soccer."

Mama didn't say a word, but she let me quit after that.

I look up at the kids peeking over the wall. What would Big Eddie have said to that dad? What about Papa? I run and pull back my leg to start an angry kick—a kick that releases my bad memory of that guy. But instead of going over, the ball thuds against the wall. The kids go nuts, laughing like hyenas—or what I imagine laughing hyenas must sound like. It's hard to stay angry when little kids are laughing like that.

I take a bow, and they giggle again. I kick, and again the ball smashes into the bricks. More titters. I'm sweating. I can hear Nita chopping, and I'm getting hungry. Still, I give the kids a little bit more of a show. I even fall over a couple of times. Totally on purpose. They laugh, and I wish I could talk to them. I try to think of Spanish words.

"Tacos!" I shout. They sputter with giggles and jabber at me while I catch my breath.

"Enchiladas!" I say. "Siesta! Guacamole!"

"Guacamole!" the kids shout back. "Tacos!" they mimic as if we're playing catch with words.

When I miss the kick again—this time not on purpose—I fold over in laughter, hardly believing that I'm speaking fake Spanish and kicking a soccer ball in Colombia. Papa's Colombia. Big Eddie's Colombia. The kids shout at me in between their giggles. Even though I have no idea what they're saying, the sound of their laughter is no different from the noise kids make in my own school. In fifth grade I sat near the window, and I liked to listen to the yelling during kindergarten recess and watch little arms navigate the monkey bars. These kids in Colombia are the same. Just kids laughing.

"Little Eddie!" a voice calls from inside the house.

I grab the ball between my sweaty palms and toss it over the wall.

"Tank you," calls the first boy in a thick accent, and the

children giggle even more. I wave as, one by one, their faces disappear behind the wall like rubber ducks at a carnival game.

My brother is standing in the doorway, shading his eyes with his hand. "Come meet Abuela."

10

AFTER THE BLINDING sun outside, it takes a
moment for my eyes to adjust. Inside the house, a dim
shape slowly takes the form of a small woman propped on
couch cushions. As my vision clears, I look for signs of cancer. Can cancer be seen? Or is it hidden, like how when
people look at me, they can't tell my father is dead?

"Eduardito," she says, her voice thin and warbly. She has
short white hair and a face so wrinkled, it looks like her
eyes are going to be sucked into the sockets. I know that
makes her sound kind of creepy-looking, but her lips are a
cheery pink, and she's wearing a sweatshirt with a picture
of a kitten on it, so she ends up looking kind of cute, like a
worn-out teddy bear that you've had your whole life.

"Ven acá, Eduardito," she says, and pats the seat beside
her. She must be talking to me. "Come." She smiles her

pink lipstick smile when the English words come out. "I don't speak English very good."

I didn't know she could speak any English, so I say, "That's okay."

"Give her a kiss on the cheek, Little Eddie," my brother says. "Un beso. That's what we do here." He's leaning against the glass patio door, watching us.

Abuela angles her face toward me. "Un besito," she says.

I do not feel like kissing anybody, much less a grandma with cancer, but I lean down and brush my lips against her cheek. It's surprisingly soft.

"You look like your papa," she says once I'm sitting next to her like she wants.

Me, look like Papa? That doesn't seem possible. Big Eddie? Sure, he's tall and dark like Papa was. No one would ever doubt that he and Papa were related. But me? I'm short, lighter-skinned. My hair isn't wavy like Big Eddie's. I shake my head.

Abuela laughs and reaches a hand toward me. She touches my mouth. "This," she says, and then she touches my chin and cheeks. "These. What is it called?"

"Mouth," I say, "chin, cheeks. They look like my dad's?"

"Exactly," she says.

"She's known our dad since he was in high school—no, younger maybe," Big Eddie says. He sits down on her other side and switches to Spanish before translating. "My parents were childhood sweethearts. That's why Abuela knew our dad so well."

"Los Eduardos," she says, and grips both of our hands in

her small ones. Hers are brown and wrinkled. Mine look pale next to them. I try to gently escape her grasp, but she has a tight grip. "Eduardo y Eduardito."

I glance over at my brother. "Eduardito?" I ask.

"It means 'Little Eddie'—only in Spanish. That's what she called me when I was little too." My brother must have more practice escaping, because he gets up and pulls a fat photo album from the bottom of a crowded bookshelf. "You want to see pictures of me? The old photos?"

"Sí, we look at photos." Abuela lets go of my hand, and Big Eddie lays the album across the rainbow-striped blanket on her lap. She points to a black-and-white photograph of a teenage boy. "Eduardo Aguado León," she says. The *D*s in this familiar name are soft like her hands. She brushes invisible dust off the picture. The boy is sitting on a beach smiling shyly at the camera. Even in shades of gray, I can tell that the sky was brilliant blue, and I can't wait to see the real beach, go swimming, catch some fish.

Abuela turns the page, and there is the same teenager again, this time seated on the sand next to a pretty teenage girl in a polka-dot bikini. "Ana María," she says. "Mi hija linda," she adds, her voice stretched like the blanket across her lap.

"That's my mom." Big Eddie runs his finger over the photo. "Like seeing a ghost."

I look from his hand to his face. "Have you ever seen a ghost?" I ask.

"Haven't you?"

I shake my head. "Ghosts aren't real."

Big Eddie and Abuela exchange glances. "If you've never seen a ghost," Big Eddie says, "how do you know?"

"Well, have you seen a ghost?"

"Sure. I've seen ghosts here in Colombia."

"Have you seen one in Minnesota?" I ask.

He shakes his head and then says, "I don't think it's as common to see ghosts there."

"Why not?"

"Maybe there isn't as much imagination. Or sorrow. It takes sorrow and a little imagination to see a ghost."

"I have imagination. Does that mean I'll see a ghost?"

Big Eddie shrugs one shoulder.

"Or does that mean ghosts are made up?" I don't say anything about sorrow. Everyone assumes I'm sad about not having a dad. But am I? Since I don't really remember Papa, I'm not sure.

"They're definitely real," Big Eddie says. "But you need to open your mind to see them. I remember a ghost I saw when I was about your age. I was with friends from school. When I pointed at the ghost, they didn't see him."

"Him?" I try to picture my brother being my age and seeing ghosts, fishing with Papa.

"Yeah, a man with a sword, maybe like the kind the Spanish conquistadores had."

"A ghost soldier?"

"Well, not exactly. Ghosts aren't quite one thing or another. I'm not sure the guy was a soldier. But he was definitely a ghost. It was sundown and we were heading back to El Centro, and I peeked down an alley and there he was.

Those other boys didn't see. Not sure if that was because they had no imagination or if they just missed him."

"What did he do? The ghost, I mean."

"Oh, nothing. Just looked at me. They're not scary. At least not in my experience."

We both stare at the photo of his mom again, and I realize he looks even more like her than he looks like our dad. It's strange too because I can see that his mom isn't anything like mine. While Ana María was tall, Mama is short, and Mama's cropped blond hair is nothing like the long ponytail in the photo of Ana María. And yet Papa married both of them. Maybe it doesn't matter so much what you look like on the outside. It's hard to imagine Papa having first one wife and one son and, later, another wife and another son. Did he love the Colombian wife and son better? Would he still have had a heart attack if he hadn't come to Minnesota? What if Papa weren't my dad? Would I still be me?

Abuela takes the album out of her grandson's hands and turns to the next page. "Yo," she says, patting her chest proudly. "Pretty, no?" She points at a picture of a woman with long black hair standing beside an arched door. Even though she's much younger, the eyes of the woman in the picture match Abuela's eyes.

"Bellísima, Abuela." Big Eddie kisses her cheek. "You were—are—beautiful."

Abuela jumps ahead a few pages in the book. There is Eduardo Aguado León looking less like a teenager and more like a man. *Like seeing a ghost.* For me, the face of my own dad in this photo album in Colombia is as strange as the idea of Big Eddie seeing a ghost in Cartagena.

In the picture, just behind Papa, I spot a petite blond woman in a flowy sundress. "That's *my* mom," I say in surprise.

My parents in the photograph are younger than they are in the wedding photo that sits on Mama's dresser. Now there are two things I can't believe: I can't believe I'm in Colombia, and I can't believe my parents were ever young like that.

Abuela leans back and closes her eyes. She coughs a rasping gasp, and I jump. Maybe that's the sound of cancer. By the time Nita comes in from the kitchen and sets a glass of juice on the table, Abuela has stopped coughing. She falls asleep with her chin bowed and her hand still gripping a tissue. The cushions are scratchy on the backs of my legs, and I want to get up, but I don't know if that would be rude. The clock on the bookshelf interrupts the silence of the living room. Next door the kids shout, and I wish I could go play soccer with them. Instead I keep flipping through the album. There are more pictures of Big Eddie's mom, some show a scruffy little dog, and others are of Big Eddie as a baby. And then there is a page filled with pictures of fish.

The ticking of the clock fades and the itchiness of the cushions eases as I examine the fish.

These are different from the fish in the picture of Papa and Big Eddie, but they're almost as big. Strange-looking fish with crooked fins and ones with lolling eyes. Fish with shiny scales and fish that look as ugly as what you might find at the bottom of a dumpster. And they are spectacular. I reach into my pocket and pull out the bronze medal. The fish with the fishing pole grins.

"Do you think we can we go fishing sometime?" I whisper to my brother, stuffing the medal back into my pocket. "I'm gonna be in a fishing tournament. Back at Lake Mad. Later this summer. Maybe you could help me practice?"

Big Eddie glances from his phone to Abuela sleeping, her mouth half-open, her breathing ragged. "Maybe," he whispers back. It's a "maybe" that sounds a lot like "probably not."

We spend most of that first day sitting on the couch with Abuela, who sleeps on and off. When she's awake, she wants to know all about my life: school, Mama, my friends. I tell her about Liam, who still hasn't texted me back, but I don't say anything about Cameron. Adults always tease kids about boyfriends and girlfriends. I tell her about going to middle school in the fall, but I don't think she understands. Big Eddie tries to translate, but I don't think he understands either.

We eat dinner at the table near the open patio doors. A breeze cools me as I eat the rice and chicken that Nita cooked. After dinner, when we're back in the living room, Nita and my brother talk in Spanish whispers. They both glance at Abuela, who's fallen asleep again, her mouth partly open, her breathing still ragged.

"Do you want to go to El Centro?" Big Eddie asks me, quiet so he doesn't wake his grandmother. "We can go there while Nita stays with Abuela."

Nita smiles and nods at me. Then he explains that El

Centro is the original Cartagena that was built with a huge wall around it to protect it.

"Protect it from what?" I ask.

"Pirates!" he says. "Well, pirates and the English invaders. Lots of invaders. Everyone wanted Cartagena. Everyone was fighting over the city."

I remember a fight I saw on the bus once. I didn't hear the beginning of the argument, but all of a sudden this kid with a striped stocking cap was getting beaten up by this other boy who always wore a black sweatshirt no matter the weather. The boy's friends were shouting, "Get him! Punch him!" and some other kids were yelling at them to stop. Liam and I didn't really know either of them, so we just scrunched down in our seat, but now I wish I had been one of the kids shouting "stop."

"Don't look so worried, Little Eddie. No one fights now. El Centro is beautiful. Like a history lesson in real life." Abuela has just awoken, and she smiles at both of us. Big Eddie turns to her. "He'll like El Centro, won't he, Abuela?"

Abuela smiles and nods. "Vayan," she says, her voice weak. "Go."

We're in the car for less than ten minutes when I see a huge gray wall that wraps around the bend in the road.

"That's the wall: La Muralla. It surrounds the original city of Cartagena." Big Eddie points while turning left and squeezing the car through a small opening in the wall. Going through the wall is like going through the car wash with the Honda at home, but when we come through, instead of blinking in the light through wet, clean windows,

I'm looking at bright buildings, colorful like the saltwater taffy I get at the state fair.

Even though it's barely six thirty, the sun has set. Unlike in Minnesota, where the summer days are long and winter ones short, it gets dark at six o'clock every night in Cartagena, Big Eddie tells me. Colombia is nearly at the equator, and here the days and nights are equal. I glance at Big Eddie in the driver's seat. Night and day. Opposite but equal. Like two brothers?

When we arrive in the center of town, the amber glow of streetlights makes me think of Christmas morning even though it's hot and sticky. Climbing out of the car, the hum of Spanish and the whisper of the ocean surround me, close like the wall. I shut my eyes and try to capture the sound so that, when I'm back in my room at home, I'll remember.

"Vámonos." Big Eddie leads me across the street and up a crowded cement ramp. I follow him to the top of a wide stone wall where dance music thrums from a café and teenagers sit around metal tables.

"When they were young, my mom and our dad used to come up here every night," Big Eddie says, looking out at the sea that is, at this time of night, a black hole. I follow his gaze, but I'm distracted by the couples nearby. Next to us, a man is seated on the low stone lip of the wall, a woman on his knee. Their mouths are pressed together in a kiss.

"Abuela said they always had their arms around each other," Big Eddie continues. We both look over at the couple, and I feel funny. I've never seen a real-life kiss up close like this. You can hardly tell where one face ends and the other begins. I wonder how they can breathe. "My mother had long black hair. Abuela used to have the same hair."

Big Eddie turns away and rubs his face with both hands. Then he suddenly crouches, posed like a sword fighter. "*En garde!* Can't you imagine the soldiers up here fighting off the pirates?"

I look away from the couple and hold out my own imaginary sword. Liam and I used to sword fight with empty paper towel rolls. We would start out banging the cardboard tubes, and then we would end up pummeling each other until we were laughing so hard that we would fall over in a heap.

After Big Eddie and I spar a few times, he sheaths his imaginary sword and leads me along the wall that protects the city and its maze of red tile rooftops and soaring palm trees. We pass more couples, groups of rowdy kids, families with small children in strollers. Vendors are selling bunches of roses and little toys that fly into the air. There's a man selling striped straw hats.

"They were together since they were as young as you," Big Eddie says. At first I'm not sure who he's talking about because I'm so busy watching the hat man. After selling one, he takes the whole stack and balances them all on his head again.

"Your mom?" I ask.

Big Eddie nods and then stops walking. "My mom loved our dad, and Abuela loved him too. That's why she wanted you to visit us. She wants to get to know you."

"I'm glad," I say in a small voice. Even though Abuela is old and wrinkly, and even though she has cancer and barely speaks English, I'm glad I'm going to get to know her, too.

I run to catch up with Big Eddie, who's ahead of me now, buying something from a cart. He hands me a little plastic dish of mango ice cream, and we sit on the steps that lead down from the wall. We eat our ice cream with orange plastic spoons shaped like miniature shovels. Big Eddie doesn't say anything more about Abuela or Papa or his mom. I look up at the black sky. The last of the mango ice cream melts on my tongue and leaves a bitter aftertaste.

11

THE NEXT DAY at lunch, Nita makes meat and more rice and smashed bananas that are called plantains. Even though I like their salty sweetness, they remind me of zucchinis, the way they look like one thing but are actually another. Between mouthfuls I ask Big Eddie again about going fishing.

"It's a lot of work, hermanito." He glances at Abuela, who's hardly eaten anything and seems to be having trouble keeping her eyes open. "I have to find a boat, fishing gear."

"What about a dock?" I ask.

But Big Eddie shakes his head. "We need a boat. It's better. How about I take you to the beach instead? It's just a couple blocks away. La playa?"

Abuela perks up. "La playa," she repeats, and grins. Big Eddie and I can't help giggling when she promptly shuts her eyes again.

"While Abuela has her nap, I'll take you to the beach," he whispers.

Abuela opens her eyes and nods approvingly. "La playa," she repeats.

It's not fishing, but it'll do. While Big Eddie helps Abuela with her medicine, I sit on the couch and pull out my phone. I tell Mama that Abuela sends her love and that Big Eddie says hi and that I'm being polite. Then I type a message to Cameron.

My brother's grandma is really sick. How's Kamp Kids?

Big Eddie collects three little white bottles filled with pills, and the blender whirrs as Nita makes a green juice for Abuela. My phone pings.

Day camp sucks without any friends. I had to bring a book to keep from dying of boredom. Did you know that fish sleep with their eyes open?

I look up from my phone when Abuela coughs again as she shuffles from the kitchen to her room. She looks at me as she passes the living room, and says, "Tos."

"Toes," I repeat, shoving my phone into my pocket. Is she talking about feet? She makes a fake coughing sound and says "tos" again. "Oh, 'tos,'" I say. "That means 'cough'?"

She smiles like I just won a gold medal. I'm starting to like this little old lady.

Once Abuela is tucked into bed for her nap, I melt in the heat as I follow Big Eddie along the sidewalk. No one else is out walking.

"It's the hottest part of the day," he says when I complain. "Everyone who can rest and relax during the afternoon does."

"Everyone here takes a nap like Abuela?"

"Not necessarily a nap, but just staying cool. Una siesta."

Siesta. I remember the scratchy blue cots and the tinkling music during nap time at Little Tykes Preschool. Then at home, the weight of Papa's warm hand on my back as I fell asleep.

I'm about to collapse on the sidewalk from the heat, when Big Eddie says, "There's el mar. The ocean."

I stop walking and gape. In some ways, the ocean looks no different from a Minnesota cornfield in winter, all flat and endless. The white sky blends into the expanse of grayish water. In one direction, two shirtless boys kick a soccer ball across the sand, and in another a bent old man steps gingerly along the shore, a large white hat shading his face. Down the beach, a woman in a brightly colored dress carries a basket on her head.

Big Eddie pulls me across the busy Avenida Santander that snakes between the neighborhood and the beach. We run across the street and keep running when we get to the sand.

"¿Listo?" Big Eddie has already slipped off his flip-flops. He piles the towels and his T-shirt on the sand. "Ready?"

"To go in? Definitely!"

It's like walking into a huge bathtub. At Lake Mad, you have to prepare yourself for cold water, even in the summer. But this is so warm, there's almost no difference between air and sea. Big Eddie is splashing in waves that surge forward and then back. The soft sand squishes with each step I take.

I'm waist-deep when something brushes against my ankle. I scream. What if it was a fish? I think of the stingrays that Mama used to see. I try to run, but the water is a wall and I fall into the waves.

"Got you!" Big Eddie's head appears above the water. He laughs and makes pinching motions with his fingers.

"Quit it!" I shout at him. Last time he came to visit in Minnesota, we went swimming at the lake. He did the same thing, attacking me underwater. I didn't think it was funny when I was eight, and I don't think it's funny now. "Don't—" I start to yell, when a horrible taste fills my mouth. I spit out the water. "Ew!" I spit some more. "Gross."

Big Eddie laughs again. "It's seawater. Salty, you know?"

I stop spitting. I knew that. Seawater is salty; lake water is not. I know lots of things. The encyclopedia says that seventy percent of the earth's surface is covered in saltwater oceans.

The water pulls me off my feet, swirls around my arms, pushes me forward, and drops me. Then a wave catches me and I'm on a roller-coaster ride inside a warm hug. Is this what it's like to be a fish? Weightless and careless, floating along? With the next wave, I kick off the sand and propel myself even farther. Big Eddie is a few feet away riding the same waves, and I forgive him for teasing me.

"Little Eddie!" my brother shouts. "Look!"

"What is it?" I sputter and spit.

Big Eddie stands chest-deep facing the great expanse that

disappears into the fading sky. The water is up to my neck here, so I grab on to Big Eddie's shoulders.

"Over there." He points to something bobbing in the water a few yards out.

It's dark and its shape reminds me of something. "It's a hat," I say. A hat floating in the water. From this distance, it makes me think of the kind of hat Abraham Lincoln wore.

"Let's get it." Big Eddie is swimming out toward it, and I try to keep a grip on him. "Hang on." When my hand slips, he says, "Careful! Don't pull down my pants."

I let go of his swim trunks. But when I kick my feet, checking for solid ground, there's nothing there. The more I kick, the more my stomach churns. What's down there? The photos of fish from the album swim past my squeezed-shut eyes.

Big Eddie grabs my arm. "We're almost there."

In front of us, riding the wave ahead, is the hat. At least, it looks like a hat. What if the hat is being worn? What if there is a person beneath the surface of the water? I get a bad feeling.

"Stop!" I yell.

Big Eddie grabs for the hat.

And then the hat—which isn't a hat at all—bobs and dips. It's a bucket, old and scratched. The kind of bucket the fishermen bring to the dock. An ordinary bucket. Big Eddie pulls it closer. He tips it forward, trying to get a good grip.

My bad feeling doesn't go away. "Don't!" I shout.

Out of the bucket, like a nightmare, comes the slosh of

dirty water and a wriggling, jiggling black cloud of leeches. Big Eddie and I screech as the leeches come tumbling out, some sinking, some floating. They brush my arms and legs as they sink into the deep water below.

The waves push us until we collapse on the shore, half panting, half laughing. Big Eddie throws himself down on the sand. "I did not expect that," he says.

"Leeches! Did you know they live on blood? Yuck!" I shudder. In the entry about leeches in my encyclopedia, it says that they feed on the blood of animals. And people. Bloodsuckers. Maybe it's not good to have so much information. I shudder again. "How does a hat turn into a bucket of leeches?"

"This is Colombia," Big Eddie says, as if this is an answer. He stands up and shakes the water off his hair like a dog.

"But it looked like a hat." I pull my knees up to my chest. "It *was* a hat."

"In Colombia," he says, holding out his hand to help me up, "anything can happen."

12

WHEN WE GET BACK from the beach, Abuela is sitting in a white plastic patio chair in the courtyard. Big Eddie kisses her cheek. She smiles and looks up at me. "How was la playa?"

I glance at my brother. He sits down on the bricks at her feet. "Little Eddie had an adventure," he says, taking her hand.

"An adventure, Eduardito? Dígame." She winks. "Tell me."

"We saw a hat turn into a bucket of leeches." I wait for her to laugh.

"Ah," she says. "That is Colombia."

"That's what he said," I say. I go to the lemon tree and test the strength of its branches. Maybe I can climb it.

"That's because that is how Colombia is, Eduardito. Do

you know surrealismo?" She looks at Big Eddie. "¿Cómo se dice?"

"Surrealism. Magical realism," he says, like he knows what the heck she's talking about.

"Yes, Eduardito," Abuela says to me in her whispery voice. "Colombia is magical. This is what we know."

I look at Big Eddie.

"Right. Magical realism is . . ." He pauses like he's looking for the right words, the words that will make me believe. "Magical things happening to real people or real things happening in magical ways."

"Like two brothers with the same name?" I ask.

"Sort of," my brother says.

"Espantos," Abuela says. "Fantasmas."

"Ghosts," Big Eddie translates.

"Ghosts," Abuela repeats, her tongue getting tangled on the *S*s and *T*.

Even though Big Eddie claimed he saw a ghost, this sounds like what my teacher called old wives' tales. And Abuela is certainly an old wife. But my brother nods. "Sometimes ghosts, and sometimes a hat turning into leeches."

"But I bet that bucket just fell off a fishing boat. That's not magic."

"That's one possible explanation. Who knows?"

I grip the lowest branch of the lemon tree. "I get it," I say. But I don't really get it. Magical hats? Ghosts? Am I supposed to believe that? My encyclopedias are full of facts. That's what's real. I know magic is just made up. One time a magician came to my school and performed. Afterward he showed us how his tricks worked. It was all about timing and distraction. Not magic.

Abuela and Big Eddie watch as I swing my leg, hooking it onto the branch. I pull myself up and hug the trunk. The scent of lemons tickles my nose.

"I used to climb that tree when I was young," Big Eddie says. "I would break the branches now."

"Eduardo planted it," Abuela says. "El árbol."

"You did?" I ask my brother.

He shakes his head. "A different Eduardo."

"Really?" I jump down. "My father?" I glance at Big Eddie. "I mean, *our* father?"

Abuela nods. "We had a mango tree long ago when my husband was still alive and the children were small. When it died, Ana María—"

Big Eddie grins like he knows where this story is going.

"Yes, tu mamá," Abuela says to him. I like how she mixes her Spanish and English words. It's like she's inventing a new language. "Ana María was so sad when the mango tree died. Eduardo was always at our house; they were so young, childhood sweethearts. Novios." She takes a deep, raspy breath and closes her eyes.

"Papa proposed to her," Big Eddie says, supplying the rest of the story. "This was after he planted a new tree as a gift to her. He pulled out the dead one, redid some of the bricks. Abuela says my mamá put on her lipstick every day and sat on the patio watching him." He laughs and then says, "When he asked her to marry him, she said yes, obviously."

Abuela smiles even though her eyes stay closed. She's

about to fall asleep. She sleeps a lot. I wonder if that's what happens when you get old. Maybe it's like practicing for when you're dead.

Big Eddie and I sit on the warm patio and listen to the faraway sound of life happening in other places. It's strange to think of Papa here in Colombia, strange to think of him anywhere else besides our old apartment in Minnesota. I clutch Papa's fishing medal in my pocket. I start to wonder what's more real—the cold disc or being here, standing under a lemon tree that he planted. Seeing Colombia makes it easier to imagine Papa having a whole life, not just the short one I remember. And that makes me sort of sad. Maybe that's why Mama never wants to talk about him; she can see his whole life.

I picture Mama at our duplex alone, Liam in New York with his new stepbrothers, Cameron at Kamp Kids without any friends, Papa's fishing gear waiting in the dark garage.

If anything is possible in Colombia, does that mean I can catch a fish?

13

ABUELA HOLDS my arm just above the elbow as we walk across the front yard to the little blue car. The children next door are getting yelled at. No matter what language, you can tell when a kid is in trouble. Remembering their little faces peeking over the wall, I guess those kids are in trouble a lot.

Big Eddie fusses around Abuela, helping her get situated in the front seat. "Tranquilo," she says, and bats his hand away when he tries to help with the seatbelt.

"You see what I'm dealing with, Little Eddie?" he says, and then leans into the car to give her a kiss on the forehead. He gently closes the door. "Jump in, hermanito."

Abuela has an appointment at the clinic, and this is the first time I'm coming along. I wonder if Abuela hates going to the doctor as much as I do. The smell, the fake smiles on the nurses, the needles alongside cartoon Band-Aids—as if that makes it better.

Abuela's clinic is loud, and people of all ages sit in plastic chairs. Men and women in white coats go in and out of two doors, one at each end of the waiting room. A woman with a yellow-and-black-striped dress sitting at a wide metal desk hands Big Eddie a clipboard. While he fills out forms, Abuela says buenas tardes to an old man across from her, and they start talking in Spanish. She smiles a lot, and he blushes. Abuela has put on extra lipstick for this appointment, and I wonder if bright colors make men like women. I think of Cameron's purple hair, and my own face flushes.

When a nurse in a white uniform comes to get Abuela, Big Eddie says to me, "You wait, okay?" He leaves me with the Spanish language magazine he was reading and follows the nurse and Abuela. I shuffle Papa's medal between my fingers as I look at the pictures of people in the magazine who wear even more lipstick than Abuela. The celebrities smile too big, and their clothes are odd. By the time I get to the ads at the back of the magazine, my brother is leading Abuela back into the waiting room.

She smiles at me and shows me a Band-Aid inside her elbow.

"What happened?" I ask. "Did you get a shot?"

"Blood," she says. "They want my blood. Like a . . ." She makes claws out of her hands and bears her incisors. "What do you call it?"

I laugh. "Vampire?"

"Sí, vampiro," she says, and then her laugh turns into a cough.

I turn to Big Eddie. "Is she okay?"

He nods and then shakes his head. "She has cancer, so she's not okay. But the doctor is going to keep her comfortable. So that's good." He looks at his grandmother the way Mama looks at me after I throw up when I'm sick. I suddenly miss Mama, and so I reach for Abuela. Her hug is surprisingly strong for an old lady.

When we get back into the car, Big Eddie says Abuela wants to go to El Centro with us.

"Sí, El Centro," she says. "Did you like it?"

I nod. "The wall is really cool. Walking on it. Super cool."

"That's all he took you to see?" Abuela swats Big Eddie on the arm. Then she turns to look at me in the backseat. "We go inside the wall. To the plaza."

"Vale," I say, and she grins.

Big Eddie drives, taking each turn in the same gentle way he helped Abuela into the car. Now that he's not driving as wildly as before, it's easier for me to watch the traffic—cars even smaller than this weave in and out, and yellow taxis honk and buses spurt black smoke. On one side of us the ocean appears, the water as endless as a snow-covered winter prairie.

"Mira," Abuela says, and points out the windshield. I lean between the front seats. We are in front of the city's impressive wall now, and in a grassy field in front of the gray bricks, dozens of people are pulling on kite strings.

In Minnesota there's a kite festival in the winter, on a

frozen lake. If the weather is just right—not too warm and not too cold—Mama and I watch the people fly kites, holding their strings in mittened hands, bright colors against the snow.

But the kites in Cartagena are even more colorful. I've never seen so many in one place. In the pink light of the setting sun, the kites dip and dance. One looks like a butterfly; one's a flower. Some are as big as the car I'm in. There's a giant squid and a whale. The kites swoop up and then dive down. They look like they're swimming.

Big Eddie turns through another opening in the wall and drives down a narrow street lined with purple and yellow houses. When we get out of the car, Abuela takes my arm again. Cigarette smoke and the smell of something raw like pee hang in the air. It's getting dark now, and I help Abuela around the big vines that grow up the sides of buildings, their branches as thick and black as snakes. I step off the curb into the street so that she won't get jostled.

Big Eddie leads the way down one street, around a corner, and along another street to a big square. There are restaurants on one side, a big white building with bars across the windows on the other. Little shops with open doors line the other two sides. Music bubbles out of the restaurant, and Abuela hums along quietly. The square is planted with trees and flowers, and I hear the splash of a fountain. In the center of the square is a statue of a man on a horse.

"Who's that?" I ask, pointing at the figure.

"That?" Big Eddie looks up. "That's Simón Bolívar, the first president of Colombia."

I look up at the bronze man. I never thought about Colombia having a president. Maybe this place is more like home than I thought.

"This is called Plaza Bolívar after him. Come. Do you want to try coconut water?" Big Eddie asks. There are little carts with hand-painted signs. One says AGUA COCO. Men and women stand by the carts selling cups of coconut water or paper wrappers of food. "Or do you want ice cream?"

"Ice cream." I grin and watch him cross the plaza to the carts. It's hot out even though the sun has set. I can feel the day's heat radiating off the buildings as if the sun has been stored in them like in a bank.

"Ice cream," Abuela repeats. "Helado," she enunciates for me.

"Eh-law-doe," I say, and she cheers.

When she starts coughing, I lead her to a bench at the edge of the plaza. We sit and I wait for her coughing to stop. I look at her arm and notice that blood has seeped through, leaving a dark spot on the Band-Aid. She sees me looking at it and folds her arms.

"You want a toy?" she asks. "¿Un volador elástico?

"A what? What toy?"

Then I see another cart where a man sells the little spinners I saw the first time I came to El Centro with Big Eddie. They shoot into the air like light-up helicopters. In the dark, the spinners fly into the sky with bright blue and pink lights like fireworks. When they float back down, a little kid runs to collect them for the man, who shoots them into the air again.

Abuela shifts next to me, and the next thing I know, she's pulling out a damp, crumpled bill. She tucks it into my hand. "You get one."

I look for Big Eddie, but I can't see which ice cream vendor he went to. I watch the spinner fly into the air and touch the sky before drifting back down. "I'll be right back."

I wave the pesos in the man's face, and he says a bunch of stuff in Spanish. After I point to a spinner, he hands it to me with a toothy smile. Back at the bench, where Abuela watches and smiles, I pull the rubber band and let go. The spinner flies into the air, just a couple of feet.

In my encyclopedia back home, there was a picture of a girl spinning a yo-yo. It was an article about physics and centripetal force. Physics—one of the forces of nature. The article had a lot of long words I didn't quite understand, but this toy spins in the same way.

When I shoot it back into the air, Abuela claps. Scooping up the spinner, I try again. It goes higher this time, and Abuela laughs. Again we watch the spinner soar into the air, and we track the light as it lists to one side. Next time I'll get it straight up. The spinner nose-dives into the grass behind us.

Even though it doesn't look like you're allowed to go into the garden that surrounds one of the four fountains in the plaza, I step over the low hedge and between two red flowering plants. My spinner is balanced on the edge of the fountain—a few more inches and it would have been in the water. I kneel and grab the toy, and pause to reach in and splash my face. But, as I'm about to stand up, a movement in the pool catches my eye.

It's a fish.

In the fading light I can make out the little waves it makes as it bumps into the wall of its home and then changes direction. I grin. "Hello, fish."

And then the fish swims toward me, looks straight at me—or as straight as a fish can look—and just stares. My hand gripping the spinner goes cold. The fish gets as close to the surface of the water as it can without leaping out. I'm still on my knees in the garden, so I'm not sure if anyone else can see this. I think of the swarm of fish that rose to the surface at Lake Mad, desperate for a strawberry from Alyssa's ice cream, and I realize the fish must think I have food. I toss a leaf into the water. Fish are so dumb; they think anything is food. But the leaf lands just behind the fish's tail, and the fish doesn't flinch. It just keeps staring at me. I'm getting creeped out now, and that makes me mad. Why does this thing keep looking at me? With my free hand I reach into my pocket for Papa's medal so that I can show the fish what we do with fish in Minnesota.

But my pocket is empty. I dig into the other pocket. Nothing.

Did I lose Papa's medal? Tears prick my eyes. I had the medal when we were at the clinic. I had it in the car. The fish flicks its tail, and the water makes soft splashing sounds. And there, in the fish's mouth, is Papa's medal. The bronze color catches the light from the plaza for a moment.

Snatching the disc from the fish's gummy jaws, I announce,

"I'm going to catch a fish." The fish in the fountain just stares up at me. "On a hook. And eat it!" The fish looks back at me, a bored expression in its glassy eyes. Then it does a little flip with its tail and swims away.

By the time I've leaped over the low hedge and skidded to a stop in front of Abuela's bench, Big Eddie is there with two ice cream bars. Abuela is sipping from a plastic cup.

"What took you so long? Did you fall into the fountain?" Big Eddie says, laughing.

"There's a fish there," I pant. "In the fountain. It took my—something of mine."

"The fountains don't have fish," Big Eddie says. "Let's see your volador elástico. I used to love playing with these." I trade my spinner for the ice cream in his hand. He stands up and expertly flicks the rubber band. The spinner goes high and straight in the air, a beacon.

"Yes," I insist, shoving cold chocolate ice cream into my mouth, "there was a fish in the fountain. And it—"

"No, fish can't survive in those fountains. Chemicals and heat. No way."

"But I saw a fish. A brown fish." Big Eddie shoots the spinner into the air again, and Abuela claps. "It stole—" I pause. Did the fish really steal Papa's medal? Or did I simply drop it? Is there another explanation?

"Hombre," Big Eddie says, shaking his head at me, "you might be a true Colombiano now."

"What do you mean?"

"Remember the hat? At the beach?"

I shudder at the thought of those leeches. I know where

he's going with this. Magic. Magical realism, I think they called it. "But this was real." I stuff the rest of the ice cream bar into my mouth, lick my fingers, and grab my brother's arm. "Come look for yourself."

Big Eddie follows me over the low hedge and toward the fountain. It's even darker now, the water barely visible. "It's right in this—"

I'm interrupted by a whistle. A man in a black uniform and fluorescent vest is saying something and gesturing, clearly telling us to get out of the garden. Big Eddie leaps back over the hedge with one step, and I scramble after him. He waves the spinner at the guard, and I hear them talking as I slide next to Abuela on the bench. She lifts her face toward the night sky, a smile on her lips. I'm panting, and I put my head between my knees, trying to catch my breath.

"Mira, Eduardito," she says, "a star."

I sit up and see a twinkle between the branches of the tree above us.

"Colombia is magical, isn't it, mijito?"

14

BIG EDDIE SITS at the dining table, papers spread out in front of him. Two lines wrinkle the space between his eyebrows.

"Can we go fishing tomorrow?" I've been waiting to ask him this. For the past two days after her doctor's appointment and our adventure at El Centro, Abuela has been in bed. The house has been quiet and kind of boring. I read my encyclopedia, played with Big Eddie's old soccer ball on the patio, and helped him move a big chair into Abuela's room. He's worried about his grandmother, and he's been having stomachaches and not eating very much, so I add, "Maybe fishing will help you feel better."

He looks up. The patio doors are wide open, and doctors' bills and hospital bills flutter in the morning breeze. An important-looking document with many pages and stamps peeks out from under forms filled in with his neat, all-capitals handwriting.

"Not now, Little Eddie."

"When?"

"I don't know." He sighs.

I plop onto the couch and try not to sulk. But if I can't go fishing, how will I be ready for the tournament? And if I'm not ready for the tournament, how will I catch a fish? And if I don't catch a fish, how will I get a medal just like Papa's? And if I can't be like Papa, how can I still be his son? How will I know who I am?

My phone pings in my pocket. I hope it's Liam. Or Cameron. It's Mama.

I heard from Big Eddie that Abuela's not doing well. You listen to your brother and don't bother him. Don't be a burden to them, ok?

I type a response promising her I'll listen. She replies right away.

Are you wearing sunscreen?

She adds a smiling sun. Since I can't roll my eyes at her, I send a thumbs-up emoji. Even though I don't even know where my sunscreen is.

When the phone pings again, Big Eddie looks up from his papers. "You get lots of messages, hermanito."

"It's just my mom," I say, reading her message.

The Honda is starting to make a strange noise. Maybe it misses you as much as I do!

"She's complaining about her car." Mama must be lonely if she's talking about the car.

"What kind?"

"Silver," I say.

"No, what kind of car?"

I feel my face get hot. "Oh, right. Honda." Next he's going to want to know how long we've had it and how many oil changes it's had.

"Nice. They run forever."

"Hers stinks and leaves puddles in the driveway. And she says it's making strange noises too."

"You have to watch the timing belt on Hondas." I wonder if Big Eddie knows this from all those magazines on his nightstand. "Has Liz changed it?"

"I'm not sure." What if my brother could fix Mama's car?

"Well, right now I need to get through these papers," Big Eddie says mostly to himself, even though I didn't ask him for anything. He straightens them into neater piles.

From the other side of the courtyard wall and through the open patio door, I hear small, shrill shrieks. "¡Americano!"

I get up from the couch and go outside.

"¿Dónde está, Americano?" A familiar brown face pops up over the bricks.

"Big Eddie," I call into the house, "what are they saying?"

Big Eddie sighs, runs his fingers through his hair, and then comes outside. "Buenos días," he says to the faces above the wall.

"¡Americano!"

"They're calling you the American."

Americano. American. Almost the same word. Only not.

"Hi!" I call up. "Do you know them?" I ask Big Eddie.

"Those are the Paredes children. Always visiting their grandparents and always making lots of noise. I think the Paredes family has been here as long as Abuela. Probably since the mango tree."

"Hola," I call to the kids. When I wave, they giggle.

"Vamos a la playa," the boldest boy says.

I turn to Big Eddie. "That means 'beach,' right? They want to go to the beach?"

"La playa," the boy repeats. He makes swimming motions with his skinny arms.

"Can I go with them?" I ask.

Big Eddie looks back at his stack of papers and then up at the little faces above the wall. "Okay. If it's all right with their grandma. But just to play in the sand." He says something in Spanish in a warning, grown-up-sounding voice. "I told them not to go swimming without an adult."

I meet the three children (who make enough noise for ten) in the front garden of Abuela's house. A woman stands on the stoop next door and waves at me. She says something in Spanish. I nod at her. I'm sure she's telling us either to be careful or to have fun—the only two things grown-ups ever say.

Like a tornado, the children pull me down the street, their little brown hands tugging at me. The bold boy is about seven, and the smaller boy and girl are both about six, maybe twins. They chatter and skip, laugh and spin, as carefree as little chickadees.

"Americano," they say. "Playa."

When we get to Avenida Santander, I make everyone

hold hands. Then we race across the street to the sand on the other side of the road.

The beach is crowded today. It's Sunday, and lots of families are having picnics under umbrellas and tents that dot the shoreline. Fathers and mothers sit in folding lawn chairs, and children run back and forth between the water and the tents, their fingers dripping with melted ice cream. Babies play at the water's edge, just like they do at Lake Mad, their chubby hands slapping the waves. The three Paredes children are already piling their flip-flops on the sand and heading toward the water.

"Wait. We're not supposed to go swimming without an adult," I call, not that they can understand me—or are listening. What about the leeches? And not only am I not wearing sunscreen like Mama wants, but I don't know if the water is safe. But she's not here and neither is Big Eddie. It's just me. Squinting in the sun, I watch the children run into the waves, their shorts and T-shirts getting soaked in seawater. Sweat drips down my back. I step out of my flip-flops and peel off my shirt. Even without swim trunks, I'm going in. We weren't supposed to go swimming without an adult, but compared to these little kids, I practically *am* an adult.

"¡Americano!" the seven-year-old shouts.

The waves splash and the sun beats down. For the first time since I got here, I feel free. I'm in charge, I'm responsible, and I don't have to worry about acting sad and respectful like I do around Big Eddie. The Paredes kids start with a chasing game that's a version of tag in the water, with me always being "it." Then the kids think it's funny to gang up on me, their little fingers scratching at my legs. When I try to get them back, they giggle and dart away, all three of them little minnows. We're laughing so hard, my mouth fills with salty water again.

One of them grabs at my leg. "Cut it out!"

The kids swim toward shore until they stand, knee-deep on their short little legs, a few feet away from me. "¡Americano!" They wiggle their skinny butts, stick out their little pink tongues.

I feel another hand on my leg. But wait.

The kids are over there. I feel it again. My heart goes flippity-floppity. What's in the water? What if it's a fish?

"Ouch!"

It hurts. My ankle. It feels like a bee sting and a skinned knee rolled into one. I'm not sure what to do, so I run toward shore. The pain comes in slow motion. Is this how a fish feels when it chomps on a lure and finds a hook in its mouth?

I make it to the sand. My ankle has swelled to an angry red. A sinking feeling lodges itself in my gut. I should never have come here by myself. Why did Big Eddie let me go?

"Come on!" I call to the kids. They wave and giggle. I motion to them. "¡Vámonos!" I try. Is that the right word for "Let's go"? It must be, because the three of them come splashing toward me. They stop when they see my red swollen ankle coated in sand like a sprinkled donut. My whole leg hurts.

The little girl grabs our shoes and my shirt while her brothers wrap their skinny arms around my waist and help me hobble back to Abuela's house. No matter how hard I try not to let them, tears stream down my cheeks and mix with the salt water.

"Aguamala," Big Eddie says after abandoning his paperwork. I'm on the floor in the living room. Abuela is sleeping in her bedroom, so we're whispering.

"What's that?"

"It's a kind of fish—what do you call it? Aguamala. You know. It means 'bad water.'"

The little Paredes kids brought me home and then scurried away in their wet clothes, clearly aware that they were going to get in trouble.

"A fish did this?" I look down at my swollen and aching ankle. Nita brings over a rag soaked in something foul-smelling.

"No, not quite a fish. Una medusa. What do you call it?" Big Eddie dabs my ankle with the rag. "Vinegar will help with the sting. It's not a fish." He sets down the rag and hooks his thumbs together, wiggling his fingers. "You know: aguamala?"

No matter how many times he says it, I still don't know what he means. My ankle—my whole leg—aches, and he keeps repeating something I don't understand. I get madder and madder each time he says it. I wish I had my encyclopedia, or a Spanish-English dictionary.

"Aguamala," he says yet again, dabbing my ankle one last time and helping me onto the couch.

I can't understand him, and he can't translate. As Big Eddie props my ankle on a pillow, I wish I were with Mama; I wish I were at home; I wish I had never come.

"Oh, yes!" he says so suddenly, my heart jumps. "Jellyfish. Aguamala."

A jellyfish? I've seen them in the tank at the zoo, all liquid and innocent-looking. They don't even look like they have teeth or a stinger. Now I wish I had my rod and a hook. A really sharp hook.

But Big Eddie is never going to take me fishing, I think as he returns to the kitchen. I pull Papa's medal from my pocket. How am I going to catch a fish if I don't go fishing? The pain in my ankle, Abuela's cancer, the jellyfish. All these things pound me like an ocean wave keeping me down.

Ping. Maybe it's Liam. I look at my phone. A message from Cameron.

Guess who's going to Kamp Kids now? Alyssa. Ugh. Did you know you can buy live bait at the hardware store?

I try to imagine Alyssa at camp. It seems odd, but not as strange as having a jellyfish sting in Colombia, I suppose.

Ugh about Alyssa. I hope your dad got you a rod. Did you know that jellyfish stings are cured with vinegar?

Before I put away my phone, I snap a picture of Papa's medal and send it to Cameron for inspiration. While I wait for it to be sent through the slow connection across the

Caribbean, I watch Big Eddie and Nita. He washes the vinegar off his hands, and she mops up the wet, sandy spot I left on the tiles.

It sure is a burden trying not to be a burden.

15

WHEN PAPA was in the hospital, Mama brought cray-
ons and paper for me so I wouldn't get bored. I sat on his
white hospital sheets and drew my family. Sticks for bodies,
sticks for arms. Huge bobble-heads with red smiles. I didn't
know he would never come home.

Now I sit with Abuela in her courtyard with her lemon
tree, and I'm not bored. I'm glad she isn't in the hospital.
I'm glad she's sitting in her white plastic chair with me next
to her. I'm glad she has my brother and Nita to take care of
her. We watch the birds flitting from the wall to the tree.
They're brown and small like the chickadees back home.

"El pájaro," Abuela says, pointing at the bird.

"El pa-pa-who," I say.

She laughs at my attempt and repeats: "El pájaro."

I try once more, and she slows down. "Pah-ha-row." I try

it again, and she reaches out, squeezes me in a hug stronger than you'd expect from an old woman with cancer.

Even after my ankle has healed from the jellyfish sting, I spend a lot of time with Abuela. And you know what? It's not so bad. Nita makes delicious empanadas, which are like little meat pies, and she teaches me how to blend a bunch of fruit with milk to make juice. I don't feel like going swimming anytime soon, but my nervousness about Colombia has faded. I love Abuela's house and her lemon tree.

"Ven acá," Abuela says to me over and over, and I bring her things, running between the kitchen and her spot in the living room and back to her bedroom. She keeps all of us busy and laughs almost as much as she sleeps.

Later, after I help Abuela inside for lunch and into her room for her afternoon siesta, Big Eddie and I sit on the concrete front porch of Abuela's house waiting for his friend Arturo. My brother is going to fix Arturo's motorcycle. Nita is already preparing dinner, and the whole house smells like fried plátanos, so it's nice to get fresh air. The front yard is planted with two pink blooming bushes and a spindly vine with purple flowers. The yard is surrounded by a short iron fence, and the street beyond it is crowded with moms and dads coming home from work, some in little cars, some in taxis, some on motorbikes.

My brother watches the traffic and says quietly, "Her breathing is getting worse." But Abuela doesn't want to go to the hospital, he tells me. "I'm glad you're here, Eduardito," he adds. My chest feels warm and my mouth wants to smile, but I know I should still show him I'm sad about Abuela. I glance at him. He's nodding at nothing, staring straight ahead. I nod too, trying to be cool like him.

Ping. I look at my phone.

Finally. A text from Liam. I open the message, but it doesn't say anything. It's a selfie of him and Clara. I don't know what to say either, so instead I take my own selfie making a fish-eyed face. I wish that we could talk. I wish I could tell him about the aguamala and the fish in the fountain. But I don't know how to begin. Liam sends one more picture, and this one includes his two stepbrothers. The three of them are smiling, and one has his eyes closed. Are those boys like friends, or "real" brothers to him? I look over at Big Eddie. Is there a difference?

I shove my phone into my pocket, and we watch the cars pass. The traffic backs up and the air fills with the smog of car fumes. Then a chugging, sputtering motorcycle comes to a stop in front of us.

Big Eddie greets the rider, who stands next to the motorcycle holding a black helmet in his hands. The two of them laugh and spit Spanish words everywhere.

"Eduardito," Big Eddie calls. "This is my friend Arturo."

"Mucho gusto," the man says, and holds out his hand.

We shake, and Arturo says, "¿Qué hubo?"

I don't know what that means, but I nod like Big Eddie does when we pass people in the street. Cool.

My brother examines Arturo's motorcycle and then grabs his toolbox from the porch. He shuffles over to the motorcycle and kneels beside it. He and Arturo talk and point, and Big Eddie is doing something that's making his hands as black as his friend's helmet.

"See, the distributor just needs to be adjusted," my brother explains to me. "Usually it's the cylinders that are misfiring." I don't understand his English words any more than I understood Arturo's Spanish. It's all foreign.

"Can you fix it?" I ask.

Big Eddie keeps twisting and shifting parts. "I fix lots of things."

Arturo sits next to me on the curb, and we watch my brother. It's like a dance, his hands moving, the fingers flicking, almost like there's music in his head as he tinkers with one part and then another. Arturo takes his phone out and starts typing. I don't know how he can look away from the performance. Big Eddie hums a tune that sounds sort of familiar. "Volverte a ver," he sings. Then he pauses to tap one hand on his thigh in a rhythm that seems to match his jangling energy.

At last he stops humming, grunts with effort, and says, "¡Eso!" as the pieces snap into place. He stands up and admires his work. "This is a Kawasaki KLR, Eduardito. Nice piece of machinery. Classic. Look at how it all fits together."

Arturo thanks Big Eddie, and Big Eddie laughs and says, "No hay problema." They punch each other's shoulders and laugh, and they remind me of me and Liam when we're just fooling around. I take a picture of the Kawasaki and send it to Liam.

Then Big Eddie switches to English and asks me, "Would you like to ride his bike?"

My eyes bug out. Ride? The motorcycle? What would Mama say? I watch as Arturo passes his helmet to Big Eddie. My brother straps it onto my head with a little leather buckle.

"Bye!" Arturo says, and sits back down on the curb.

"Do you know how to drive this?" I ask my brother.

"Of course!"

The motorcycle leaps to life. I back up from the cloud of exhaust, but Big Eddie is tilting forward, almost as if he wants to drink in the smell of the engine. Straddling the bike, he looks happier than he has since Abuela started having more trouble breathing.

"Get on."

I climb on behind Big Eddie and hold on to his waist as tightly as I can. We take off, and over the roar of the motorcycle, he cries, "¡Epa!"

I am not yelling with joy like him—at least not at first. As we lean into the first corner, the concrete of the road seems to come closer than I'd want. Then we straighten out and head onto Avenida Santander. The smell of seawater mixes with the fumes of gasoline. The wind whips at my arms, and I hold on tighter. I'm scared but brave. A smile stretches its way across my face. I feel like the spinner when it swerved and spun through the night air of the plaza.

Even after we return Arturo's motorbike and he chugs away, I still feel like we're zooming around. Big Eddie looks like he just rode the biggest roller coaster at the Valleyfair amusement park. I feel like I just faced death and survived. Luckily, Abuela is awake and sitting on the sofa when we come into the house, because the two of us can't stop laugh-ing and whooping.

"¡Hola, mi abuelita!" Big Eddie says, leaning down to kiss her cheek. "¿Cómo te sientes?" She nods and smiles. She's always refreshed after her siesta. "¿Quieres música?" he asks.

"Claro, mijo," she says. "Music!"

"Listen to this, hermanito." Big Eddie taps his phone, and a song blasts out. He starts to sing the same tune he was humming in the street.

"I've heard that song before," I say as he moves his hips to the beat.

"It was Papa's favorite song. It's called 'Volverte a ver.' That means . . ." Big Eddie pauses. "It means 'to see you again.'" He sings a little.

And as he sings, even though I can't understand the words, I hear Papa's scratchy voice singing the same song, and I picture him dancing in the living room of our apart-ment. It's my own memory of him. I reach into my pocket and clutch Papa's medal.

"It's by the Colombian singer Juanes," Big Eddie says. "Do you like it?"

I laugh as he grabs me by the arms and swings me in a big circle. "It's a good song," I say when he releases me.

"Ahh," Big Eddie cries. "You're a true Colombiano. And now, we dance la cumbia!"

"What's 'cumbia'?" I ask.

He clicks to a different song, and a fast, pulsing beat comes bouncing out of the little speakers.

"¡La cumbia! It's Colombia's dance. Así." He begins to

step in and out, making little turns in the middle of the living room, and I see Papa all over again. The music is Big Eddie's on-off switch, and I picture Papa dancing like this in my bedroom when I was supposed to be going to sleep. Another memory.

Now Abuela claps and laughs too. "¡Anda!" she cries.

My brother dances in circles around me. It's sort of embarrassing. I have no idea what I'm doing, but I laugh and try a little anyway. Big Eddie stands in front of Abuela and holds out his hand, bowing. She takes it, and he pulls her up gently. They move to the music, Big Eddie holding his grandmother as her tiny slippered feet follow the beat.

And then something terrible happens.

"¡Abuela!" Big Eddie cries out. There's a strangled sound in his voice.

I don't know how, but suddenly Abuela is on the floor. Her face is white like the tiles. Big Eddie's is green. She leans on him as he helps her into her bedroom. Is she hurt? Is she in pain like I was when I got stung by the aguamala? If only we could fix her with a little vinegar.

I hover outside her room. "What happened?" I whisper, trying not to be a burden.

Big Eddie glances at me. "Not now," he says.

I go out to the patio, where I won't be in the way. The kids next door are quiet. A breeze that smells like salt water blows. Life is something. One moment we're dancing the cumbia in the living room. And the next? The next moment, everything can change.

· ✳ · ✳ ·

Big Eddie comes into the courtyard and stands beside me. Somewhere a television blares, and even though the words are in Spanish, I can tell by the loud music and excited talking that it's a commercial.

"I called the doctor," Big Eddie says, his voice rough and bruised. "He'll come in the morning."

I nod.

Big Eddie squeezes my shoulder and then goes back inside.

Ping. I look at my phone. I hope it's Liam.

It's not.

We had a cold snap here. Fifty-five degrees yesterday—in July! Are you having nice warm weather?

I realize that Mama doesn't know. It makes Minnesota feel very far away. I reply.

Abuela fell this afternoon. She's ok but the doctor is coming tomorrow. I'm trying not to be a burden.

The phone pings again. Mama replies, **Oh no,** and includes a crying face.

I tell her it's sad here.

Do you need anything? Is she ok? Does Big Eddie want you to leave? I'll call him.

I start typing a reply, but I don't know what to say. Will he want me to leave? My cheeks are wet when I put my phone back into my pocket. It must be the humidity here in Cartagena.

A doctor comes to check on Abuela the next morning, and the whole time he's here, I stand outside her door like one of the soldiers on the wall protecting Cartagena. The doctor has a mustache like Papa's, and he wears a white coat and carries a black bag like he's in a TV show. He sets up a machine that has tubes going into Abuela's nose. After he leaves, Big Eddie explains what's happening. The doctor said that Abuela's cancer is making her very sick, that she needs help breathing, that she doesn't have long. She doesn't want the medicine that will make her cancer go way, because it won't make the cancer go away forever, and first it will make her feel worse.

"Chemo?" I ask. I read in my encyclopedia that chemotherapy is a medicine that's used to treat cancer. "Can't you make her take it?"

Big Eddie doesn't answer.

"When you say she doesn't have long, do you mean she's going to . . ." I can't quite ask what I want to ask.

Big Eddie just shakes his head.

16

WHEN MAMA and I lived in the apartment, our front door opened into a stinky corridor with flickering fluorescent lights and dirty carpeting. My favorite thing about the new duplex is that our door opens to the outside, where I can sit on the step. Now I sit on Abuela's front step, watching the traffic in front of the house, which is more interesting than anything I see in Minneapolis. Neighbors walk by pushing carts from the market and leading lazy dogs that pee in the shrub across the street. I watch the cars: the ones that drive fast, their black-tinted windows tightly shut, and the ones that go slowly, trailing music behind them. All different kinds of people ride noisy motorbikes—young men, old ladies, small children with pink backpacks. I don't spot a Kawasaki KLR. A donkey pulls a rickety cart. Three teenage girls in matching pleated skirts walk past. None of them have purple hair.

I go back into the house, shutting the heavy front door behind me. Big Eddie went to the bank, something to do with hospital bills, and Nita is washing clothes. It's just me and Abuela.

"Ven acá, Tito," she calls weakly as I walk past her room. Ever since she fell, she's been spending all her time in her room, where the oxygen machine makes a constant and pulsing whooshing sound. Her skin is even grayer, and her phlegmy cough seems endless. She's been calling me "Eduardito" since I arrived, but now she calls me "Tito," a nickname in Spanish. Tito. Not "Little," not "Big." Tito. A name all my own.

"Hola," I say to Abuela in a soft voice. I know I don't sound like a Colombian. But Abuela's face always brightens at my Spanish. The machine that helps her breathe thrums. I sit in the chair next to her. Now that she's stuck in bed, she wants someone to be near her at all times. It may sound kind of sad to stay by a sick old lady, but it's nice. Calming. Cozy.

"Hello," she says with an emphasis on the *H* as if it's going to escape if she doesn't grab it. She coughs, and her whole body shakes, the bed vibrating. My face makes a frowning shape even though I try not to let it. I hand her the little glass of water from next to the bed. Abuela smiles and pats my arm. "No te preocupes. Do not worry," she says.

And more things. She lies back on the pillows and talks and moves her hands and coughs. The plastic tubes going into her nose don't slow down her talking. I'm not sure what she's saying, but it feels like the most important thing in the world to listen to her.

Abuela takes my hand. "Tito," she says, "you are a good boy."

Her fingers are cold but so soft, the knuckles creased. She squeezes my hand. I never knew that old people could be so soft. They look so wrinkled and crusty.

In Minneapolis there's an old man who sits on a bench by the dock at Lake Madeline. He's there all the time watching the fishermen. Maybe he lives there. He's always on the same bench, his hands folded around a cane propped between his knees. He wears a flat newsboy hat, and his head shakes like a bobble-head. He never smiles, never talks to anyone. Kids at school say he'll hit you with his stick if you get too close. His face is red and peely. When you walk by, you can smell something worse than dead fish.

Abuela never smells bad, and her wrinkles make her look like a little doll.

"Tito," she says again, and I decide to show her something.

"Abuela," I say. "Look." I pull the metal disc out of my pocket. I toss it into the air. Toss, catch. It's like a coin. Heads or tails. "This was my dad's."

She sits up straighter. I place the fake-bronze medal in her hand.

"¿Qué dice? What does it say?"

"'Second Annual Arne Hopkins Dock Fishing Tournament.'" I flip it over. "'Eduardo Aguado León.' Third place for fishing."

"Tu papá." She smiles when she says "your father." I hope Mama will smile just like that when I win my own medal. "¿Eduardo lo ganó?" she asks. "He won it?"

"Yep. And I'm going to win this same contest when I get back to Minnesota. I'm trying for first place, but third place is pretty cool too."

She studies the picture of the fish with the rod, and a laugh belts out of her. "Fish is fishing?"

I laugh too. "It's funny, isn't it?"

She points at the dresser.

"Do you need something?"

"You get it for me, Tito."

I open the top drawer. She shakes her head vigorously, and I shut it, but not before I see lace and silky cloth and neatly folded squares of white cotton. Old lady underwear—yikes. This time, instead of opening, I point. "This one?"

She shakes her head again. When I point to the bottom drawer of the dresser, she says, "Sí. Yes." I pull the drawer open. It's heavy, packed with worn notebooks and loose pictures and more photo albums. A library of memories, like the boxes in the garage at home. I pull out the albums one by one and pile them on the floor next to the bed.

When I stack a deep red album on top of the others, she gets excited and says, "Yes, yes, Tito." She holds out her arms to me. "Dámelo, mijo."

I put the album on her lap. It's so thick, I'm afraid it'll crush her skinny little legs. Each plastic page makes a crinkly sound as she turns it. I catch glimpses of yellowed photographs of blurry, smiling faces.

While she's turning pages, my phone pings.

Have you gone fishing yet? Alyssa and I went to fireworks last night. Super cool.

Fireworks? I check the date on my phone. July fifth. That means I missed the Fourth of July. And that there's just a few weeks until the tournament. While Abuela turns pages, I text Cameron back.

Sorry you had to spend 4th of July with the Schmidt kids.

I add a tongue-sticking-out face. Almost immediately, my phone pings again.

It was fun.

Cameron and Alyssa? I stuff my phone back into my pocket without texting back.

Abuela is turning the pages faster and faster. She's looking for something. Then she pulls apart the plastic sheet with a ripping noise, peels off a photograph, and hands it to me: the same picture I found in the garage. A man, a boy, a fish. The biggest fish. This copy is less worn, its corners smooth and flat. I hold it closer and stare at the smile lines in my dad's cheeks. The pattern in my brother's striped shirt. The blank stare of the fish's eyes.

"Tito," she says. And coughs. Her cough sputters like the Kawasaki. "Tu padre, Eduardo Aguado León. Brother. Eduardo," Abuela says hoarsely, stabbing the photo with her knobby index finger. "Fish," she says, only it sounds like "fiss."

She tucks the photo between two pages of the album before turning to another picture. This one is of a beach. Three adults and one baby crowd onto a plaid blanket. A striped umbrella shades the baby boy, who is clearly Big Eddie.

Before he was big.

"La playa." Abuela holds the photo. "We used to take Eduardito to la playa when he was a baby. Every Sunday. Picnics on the sand. All you need in the world is tu familia. And some pan de bono, fresh juice, chicken." She titters. "You eat lots of sand with your chicken at a picnic, no?"

I smile in response.

"Every Sunday, always. Me, Ana María, Eduardo, and your brother. We would have taken you too, Tito. A la playa."

Even though I know what that means, she adds, "Beach." Only, the word that comes out of her mouth sounds like a swear word. I swallow a little giggle. She doesn't know why I'm laughing, but she joins in, and then her laughter turns to coughing. At last her lungs seem to calm down, and she says, "We go."

I nod, even though I'm not sure where she thinks we're going.

"We go to la playa, Tito." She looks from me to the photograph of her family on a picnic. "Yes, you take me to la playa, mijo."

Wait. She wants to go to the beach? I listen to the machine helping her breathe, I study her pale face and thin body. She doesn't look like someone who's going to the beach. I begin to shake my head.

"¿Cuándo?" Her eyes are sparkly like that star she pointed out to me at the plaza. "When do we go?"

I don't know when or how, but I decide right then that I am going to get Abuela to the beach.

"Soon, Abuela," I say. If Abuela can give me my own

name, I can give her a trip to the beach. No matter how many jellyfish are out there, I will bring her. I know I'll need Big Eddie's help, and I'm not sure he'll like the idea. He reminds me of Mama, so overprotective. Abuela coughs again. I know she's sick, but that's why I'm going to take her to the beach. When you're eleven, you never get to do what you want, but when you're old like her, you should be able to.

She takes my hand as if she needs to hold on to something. Her cough ripples through to my own chest. And I realize two things: Even though she's not *my* abuela, she's the closest thing I'll ever have to a grandmother.

And she's dying.

17

PAPA HAD A scratchy chin and a round belly. He used to give me rides on his shoulders, and the whole world looked different from up there. Whenever I saw his large brown work boots next to the front door, I knew he was home, and I would listen for his response when Mama called "Eduardo!" from across the old apartment, a smile in her voice.

And then there was the hospital bed, the white sheets. Did Papa make a sound when he died? I wasn't there. Was he afraid? Was he in pain? Who is in more pain—the person who dies, or the people they leave behind?

I'm sitting next to Abuela's bed holding her hand again while I ponder these things, and also how to get her to the beach.

Over the last week we've been taking turns sitting with

Abuela. We listen to the coughs, the breathing machine, and the traffic outside her window. Me, Big Eddie, even Nita. When it's Nita's turn, Big Eddie takes me somewhere close by. We went to the market, where I saw huge stacks of mangoes and pineapples and drank fresh coconut lemonade. We picked up fried chicken at Kokoriko, a fast-food restaurant that gives you disposable plastic gloves for eating your wings and drumsticks. Big Eddie says "kokoriko" is what a rooster says in Spanish. He smiled when I repeated it. It was nice to see him smile, so I said it three more times. I haven't asked Big Eddie about taking Abuela to the beach, but he took me twice. He sat on the sand and watched me jump in the waves. Every time I laughed, I felt bad, like I shouldn't be having fun.

Neighbors and old friends also come to sit with Doña Ana María, as they call her. She takes their hands when they bend down to kiss her cheek. While visitors are there, my brother stands outside her bedroom door like a bodyguard, his face pinched with sadness. It reminds me of Mama and her sadness that I never really understood but wished I did.

Mama used to sit on the edge of my bed when I was in kindergarten and say, "I'm sad, Little Eddie-boy. I miss your papa." I felt sad too. But not because I missed him.

Because, except for those work boots and a couple of songs he liked, I hardly remembered him. I hardly knew him. I only had four years with him, and those years when you're little don't really count. But maybe by competing in the Fourteenth Annual Arne Hopkins Dock Fishing Tournament, I'll learn something I didn't know about Papa. About me.

And now, I wish I could know Abuela better. Even though she's still alive, I feel sad because there's so much I don't know about her. I wish I could know how she feels, what her life was like, what will happen to her next. I wish I could know everything.

At the sound of the front door opening, I slide my hand out of Abuela's limp grasp and sneak out of the bedroom.

"She's sleeping," I whisper to my brother, who's carrying groceries.

Big Eddie peers around the doorway at his grandmother. "Thanks for sitting with her, Little Eddie," he whispers back.

I follow him into the kitchen, where he dumps plastic grocery bags onto the counter. "I bought ingredients for coconut rice." Nita begins unpacking the food. "Nita uses my mother's recipe." Big Eddie and Nita speak in rapid Spanish as she fills a pan with water. "You have to try coconut rice before you go back to Minnesota," he says.

My flight home is in eight days. Mama keeps texting Big Eddie, asking if I should come back early or if she should come here or if she should ask the university for another deferment. He doesn't seem to know what he wants. I don't know what will happen. No one does.

I look at the coconut and the huge bag of rice. I take a deep breath. "We have to take her to the beach."

"Abuela?" he asks, as if I might be talking about Nita

wanting to go. "She can't. Besides, she's too sick to know what she wants, Little Eddie." Even with a short laugh and a smile, his despair shows through.

"She does. She wants to go to the beach. And I want to be called Tito."

"You need to leave this to me. ¿Vale?"

It's not okay. "But she should go if she wants to. Like you did when you were little? On a picnic?"

He closes the refrigerator door. "It's too risky."

"Only to the beach and back?"

"No." Big Eddie's big voice is at odds with the quiet house. He slams the door to the patio and stands in the shadow of the lemon tree. A match flares and he lights a cigarette. I watch it move from his mouth and back again. Gross. I didn't know my brother smoked. So many things I don't know.

"Big Eddie?" I open the patio door and stand not quite outside, not quite inside. I feel small. Little, like my name.

Big Eddie doesn't turn around.

"Just let me think." His words are as sour as the lemons in the tree. "I can't think." He sounds mad the way Mama gets mad sometimes. Mad and sad go together.

I leave him and sit on the front step. I pick up my phone. Still nothing new from Liam, but there is a message from Cameron:

Alyssa told me about the salad bar in middle school. Did you know that the eighth graders spit in the lettuce?

Now I feel mad and sad too. Who cares about salad bars or eighth graders or Alyssa? I answer Cameron:

Are you best friends with Alyssa now?

She doesn't reply. Silence from her and Liam and Big Eddie.

"Little Eddie." A scratchy whisper. "Eddie!"

I pull the pillow over my head to block out the noise.

"Little Eddie! Ed! Eduardito! Tito!"

At the sound of my new name, I snatch the pillow away and open my eyes. It's dark, but I can see Big Eddie standing over me. He stayed silent all through Nita's meal of coconut rice, a thick dish with blackened bits of sweet coconut milk. It looked as strange as some of the foods Mama makes, but when I tasted it, I discovered that coconut rice is better than anything from Mama's kitchen. I ended up eating my whole serving and asking for seconds.

"Wake up. I need your help." He's wearing shorts, a T-shirt, and his big sneakers.

"What time is it?"

"It's four."

"In the morning?"

"I need your help. Get dressed."

"What's the matter? Is it Abuela?"

"She's okay, Little Eddie. But I decided something. I need your help."

I get dressed and slip my feet into flip-flops. In the living room Abuela is on the sofa, wrapped in the striped rainbow blanket. She smiles and waves for me to come nearer.

Should I say good morning? I'm not sure if four a.m.

counts as morning. "¿Buenos días?" I say, more like a question than a greeting.

Big Eddie is in the kitchen filling a grocery bag with bread, three cups, and another blanket. Beside the bag is a plastic pitcher of juice.

"What's going on?" I sit next to Abuela and pat her leg. "What's the matter with Abuela?"

"We're taking her to the beach," Big Eddie says firmly.

"Now?"

She smiles, but her breathing is loud and crackly. Her face, even in the dim light coming through the glass door, is so pale, it's almost blue. She takes my hand, and her fingers are ice.

"La playa," she says, and grins wide.

18

I HAVE NO IDEA where my brother found a wheelchair, but there it is on the sidewalk, in the dark.

"You changed your mind?" I ask him. "Where did you
get the wheelchair? Why are we going in the middle of the
night?"

"Sometimes you have to do things right when you want
to do them. There isn't always time to think about it."

"But you said no yesterday."

Big Eddie looks at Abuela, who is supporting herself in
the doorframe as we get the wheelchair ready. "You were
right, Little Eddie. She wants to go to the beach. She should
go to the beach."

Abuela holds on to my arm as we come down the front
step. She hobbles, one foot in front of the other, and then
pauses to rest. Big Eddie lowers his grandmother into the

chair. The sound of techno music pulses in the distance, and I wonder who is still up dancing at four in the morning.

"Vámonos," Big Eddie says, and hands me the sack of food and the pitcher.

Abuela says something, and we both lean down to hear her better. "Beach," she says again, her voice crackling. It still sounds more like a curse word. Big Eddie and I look at each other and giggle. It feels good to laugh with Big Eddie the way we used to when he came to visit—when he would tickle me and take me to the park. Now Abuela laughs with us until her laughter turns to coughing.

When we arrive at the beach, the sand is dark in the moonlight. The umbrellas the beachgoers usually rent have been folded up, leaving the shore empty. In between coughs, Abuela's face spreads into a wide smile.

"Can you help?" Big Eddie struggles with the skinny rims of the wheelchair in the sand. The two of us push, but the wheels sink farther like it's quicksand instead of regular sand. "I'll carry it." Big Eddie lifts the front of the chair while I push from behind.

Abuela rasps. He sets down the wheelchair and kneels in front of his grandmother, who is trying to say something. "It's worth trying," he whispers, and stands up. I already know he would do anything for Abuela, so I'm not surprised by how determined he is. And if he is, I am too.

"Let's try it without the chair," Big Eddie says. "We can do it, don't you think?"

I like the way he says "we."

Abuela weighs almost nothing, but she's as difficult to

grab a hold of as a slippery fish. She clings to my elbow, and we half carry and half drag her along.

We make it to the edge of the water, where our shadows in the moonlight hang in front of us like they can't wait to get to the ocean. Ahead, the sea is a blank canvas, as black as the night sky. Nothing. It's like looking at nothing. I wonder if the fish know it's night. Do fish really sleep with their eyes open? I wish I had my encyclopedia, but the D-E-F volume is far away, stacked on my desk in my room in Minnesota.

Big Eddie lays the blanket down at the water's edge, and we lower Abuela onto it. He pours cups of juice from what's left in the pitcher after all the sloshing. Every time a car drives past on the road behind us, I can't help turning around. It feels like we're doing something illegal.

"A nadar," says Abuela. She speaks around her breaths like a tiger moving through trees in a jungle.

Big Eddie laughs and squeezes her hand.

"What does she want?"

"To swim."

"Okay," I say. If Abuela wants to swim, she should swim.

"But— Oh, okay." Big Eddie gently pulls off Abuela's pink slippers, and she smiles as her feet touch the sand.

"Arena," she says, grinning at me.

"What?"

"Arena," she repeats.

"'Arena' means 'sand,'" Big Eddie interprets.

"Ah-rain-ah," I repeat. Sand. I rub my palm across it, still warm from the day.

We try to help Abuela stand, but she says something and bats away our hands. "Agua, mijos."

"She says it's okay," Big Eddie says. "She just wants you to bring her some seawater. For her feet."

I dump out the last of the juice. It makes a river in the sand heading toward the ocean. At the water's edge, I try to fill the pitcher without stepping into the black water. The ocean seems different at night, creepier, scarier. I don't want to meet any aguamalas in the dark. Or leeches. I check the pitcher—no water. I look back at the little shape on the sand: Abuela waiting for seawater. I have to get Abuela what she wants. I splash in, and the waves coat my legs. After filling the pitcher, I run back.

Big Eddie's arm is around Abuela. She looks cold even though the night is almost as hot as the day. Each inhale and exhale she takes is like the water lapping at the shoreline— barely touching, then pulling back.

I pour water onto her bare feet. The sand darkens. She wiggles her toes in the puddle. "More. Más."

I pour the rest of the water onto her feet.

She smiles at me. "Más," she says.

"Más," I repeat. Another word for my collection.

I fill the pitcher again. I'm not thinking about aguamalas or leeches. I just know I have to get water to Abuela. Each time I pour it onto her feet, she sighs with something between pain and pleasure. It's exactly how I feel.

Later, after we bring Abuela home and tuck her into bed, I dream about a boat. In the dream I'm balancing on the railing like on a tightrope. On one side is black water like the sea at night. On the other, the floor of the boat is piled with slimy, dead jellyfish. I'm about to fall—I'm not sure which way—when I jerk awake. It's daytime. Big Eddie's bed is a tangle of sheets. A box of tissues is mixed up in them like a sailboat on ocean waves.

I climb out of bed and pull on my shorts, checking the pocket for Papa's medal. When I get to the kitchen, the bright midday sun blinds me. I squint. Something feels different, but I can't tell what it is. A plate of fruit waits on the counter, probably for me. The clock on the bookshelf ticks as usual. I hear Nita doing laundry in the little room out back. But there is a silence, an emptiness. I bring the plate of papaya into the courtyard and sit on the warm bricks. I'm used to the heat now. Maybe that's my Colombian side. The Paredes kids next door shout, but no soccer ball comes flying.

"There you are." Big Eddie appears in the courtyard. His eyes are rimmed in red, and his chin is black with an unshaved beard. My throat clenches.

And I know what's wrong. But I don't want to know.

"That was fun last night," I say. Loud. Louder than I need to be. "The beach at night was so . . . and the way Abuela says 'beach,' it's pretty funny—"

"I have to tell you something, Little Eddie." He sits in the plastic patio chair. Abuela's chair.

If he doesn't tell me, then it can't be true.

"I've never been to the beach at night. It was so cool. Don't call me 'Little Eddie,'" I say, because I don't want him to tell me anything. "I'm Tito now."

"Little Eddie, please listen."

"I'm going to send Mama a message and tell her about the beach. The way Abuela wiggled her—" I'm crying, and Big Eddie is too. "She's gone, isn't she?"

Big Eddie only nods. When he stands up, the plastic chair tips over backward, making a quiet thud on the bricks. He doesn't pick it up. He puts his large hand on my head, and I never want him to move it. The weight hurts my neck, and the hurt feels good.

"After you went to bed." He sits down next to me on the bricks, and the top of my head still feels warm from where his hand was. "She was smiling. Coughing. And then . . . Mi abuelita."

The sound Big Eddie makes is so terrible, I want to run. I want to run and hide under the hot blankets. Big Eddie needs me. And so, just like I do with Mama when she's sad, I put my hand on his arm and listen to him sob. *Nothing*, I think, *will ever be right ever again.*

19

THAT NIGHT, Big Eddie and I fall into our beds in the room across the hall from Abuela's closed door. Our sadness fills every crack and crevice of the house and it seeps into the patio. My brother is exhausted from planning the funeral, and I'm worn out from not being able to help him. He falls asleep almost instantly, and then I'm asleep too.

In the middle of the night, I wake.

What was that sound? Was it breaking glass from the bottles Big Eddie lines up at the door? A thief? I can barely see my feet as I swing them out of bed. I feel creaky and sore from all the crying yesterday. I make out the shape of my brother sleeping across from me. Maybe the sound I heard was just Big Eddie's snores filling the darkness. Not a burglar.

I'm glad he's sleeping. After he made phone calls and

arrangements for the funeral, Big Eddie wandered around the house. He didn't cry much, but he kept sitting down and then standing back up. I called Mama, and she wanted to talk to him. I sat on my bed while he was on the phone and listened to them discussing the university. At first Big Eddie argued, his accent becoming stronger as he listed excuses. Then he was quiet, finally nodding into the phone and saying, "Yes, Liz. You're right, Liz." They decided he's going to start in the fall semester as planned, so he'll fly back to Minnesota with me. I won't be an unaccompanied minor this time.

I tiptoe over yesterday's clothes and the balled-up tissues on the floor and quietly creep into the hall. I do not look at Abuela's closed bedroom door.

In the kitchen I don't have to turn on the lights because the moon shines through the windows. I pour water from the jug in the refrigerator and hold the glass against my sweating forehead.

I'm wide awake now, so I pull open the doors to the courtyard. Being outside in the middle of the night reminds me of our picnic with Abuela, and I have to swallow hard.

Then there's the sharp sound again. Is it a rooster's crow? I look up. The black sky glitters with stars. Above me a lemon hangs from a branch of the tree, as round as the moon. I reach up. I want to bring one home in my suitcase. The leaves rustle as I tug on the fruit.

And there, sitting in the crook of a tree limb, is a figure.

I blink. I'm tired. Upset. I must be imagining things.

The figure shimmers. Is there a person up there? In the

middle of the night? I remember Big Eddie's glass bottles lined up at the door. Did someone get around them or climb over the wall? Would a burglar sit in a tree? I shut my eyes, squeeze them closed. I hear a noise, different from the first, and this time I know it's not a rooster crowing.

I open my eyes and there it is. Not it. Her. Still in the branches. The ghostlike figure is a woman. A woman with long black hair, almost to her waist, and a smile that makes me want to smile back even though I'm pretty sure I should be afraid right now, but I'm not. Because the woman has eyes exactly like Abuela's. She's wearing a long skirt and a blouse that's white and shimmery, with fluttery sleeves. Her eyes sparkle in the same way Big Eddie's do, especially when he's about to play a trick on me.

The ghost Abuela looks up at the stars just like she looked up that night at the plaza. Then she looks back at me.

Abuela and Big Eddie said that Colombia is a magical place, that hats turn into leeches, that there are ghosts. Even though I saw a fish steal Papa's medal, I still didn't believe them, but now there is something magical right in front of me.

She blows me a kiss, letting it fall off her fingertips and float down through the leaves of the lemon tree. Now, I know a kiss isn't a thing you can see, but I swear this kiss—this pinprick of light—leaves her hands and flies through the night air until it lands on my cheek.

I wake up on the couch in the living room. Big Eddie is standing next to me holding a mug of hot chocolate. His face looks puffy, but he has shaved his stubble. Nita is scrambling eggs for our breakfast as if it were a normal day. I can't believe I slept through all that racket.

"Rough night?"

I sit up and take the mug. The chocolate is sweet and thick. I'm achy the way I used to be after a soccer match, and my head feels fuzzy and—the ghost. Should I tell Big Eddie?

"I used to sleepwalk when I was younger, especially when I was upset," Big Eddie says, sitting beside me. "Is that what happened?"

The white parts of my brother's eyes have red streaks, and the skin on his face sags. I don't know if telling him I saw a ghost of Abuela will cheer him up or make him sadder.

"Just couldn't sleep," I say.

"Lo siento, hermanito," Big Eddie says.

Then I do something crazy. I lean toward my brother, wrap my arms around his neck, and leave an awkward, brotherly kiss on his cheek.

It feels just as enchanted as Abuela's.

20

BY THE AFTERNOON, Abuela's little house is filled with people. She—well, her body—is in a casket in the middle of the living room on the coffee table. Nita makes pot after pot of dark, black coffee, and in between pouring the boiling water over the coffee grounds, she washes cups.

The room echoes with the sounds of tinkling china and whispered cries. "Lo siento," the visitors say. They are mostly as elderly as Abuela, old friends with white hair. Some of them I recognize from when they came to sit with her. Big Eddie's friend Arturo arrives on his chugging motorcycle, and the Paredes family from next door come—the kids suddenly shy behind their grandparents. Old ladies that Big Eddie says are Abuela's cousins pinch my cheeks and say things I don't understand. I think of the fish at the fountain at the plaza; I feel as out of place as it looked.

The mourners arrive with their arms spread open and trap Big Eddie in hugs, in corners, in conversations. I want to ask him how he's doing. I want to ask him about the beach and if we did the right thing by bringing Abuela there. At the same time, I want to be alone, curled up in my bed with one of Big Eddie's Spanish car magazines, but I have to stay in the living room next to Abuela-only-not-Abuela. I start to hate the words "lo siento" and also the scent of the squishy ladies whose grasps I can't escape.

I think it can't get any worse, but then we all go to the church. This is worse. Sadder. Lonelier.

The church is strangely cold, and it's a relief after the sweaty walk from the house through the afternoon sun. Big Eddie and I sit on hard wooden benches, and in front of us a man in a dress (a priest, Big Eddie tells me) speaks in Spanish, using words that I haven't learned yet. The church smells like damp concrete and rancid perfume. There's standing and sitting and kneeling. Up, down. The priest talks, shouts, mumbles. I'm so tired, my eyes burn. When I look at the cross hanging on the wall, I see it sway first to the right, then to the left. The casket that men carried to the church seems to be wobbling. The stone walls breathe in and out. I blink hard, and the movement stops.

Then I blink again and start to cry. Not like when I was a little kid and I got mad because I didn't want to go to bed. This is a different kind of crying. My cheeks are wet. A drop plops onto my lap, but no sound follows. Next to me Big Eddie's mouth is closed so tightly, his lips almost disappear. His eyes are dry, but his shoulders are shaking. It's as if my eyes are doing the tears and his body is doing the weeping. It's like I'm part of my brother and he is part of me, and then I think I'm going to faint even though I don't know what that feels like.

And then I know I'm going to throw up.

I squeeze past Big Eddie's shuddering body and run down the center aisle, my shoes clapping on the stone floor. Behind me, the murmur of concerned voices is like the wake behind a boat. I'm not sure where the bathroom is in this church, but the doors open into a garden, where I spot a few pink flowers at the base of a palm tree. That's where I puke up the eggs Nita made me eat this morning, and the green juice and the pineapple.

When I'm done, I sit on the steps at the front of the church and think about Abuela. Before today, I'd never seen a casket. I'd never been to a funeral before. Well, that's not true. I remember a blue button-down shirt, a stuffy room, Mama clutching my hand—at what I now realize was Papa's funeral. I'm thinking about how scratchy the collar of that shirt was, when Big Eddie, followed by the others, leaves the church.

When he see me, he stops. "Are you okay?"

"Are you?"

He takes my hand and pulls me into a hug.

Later, after the guests from the funeral have left Abuela's house and the living room is silent, Big Eddie flops onto the couch. At first everyone was crying, dabbing their eyes, holding each other tight enough to strangle a person. But when the sun set, the funeral became a party.

I thought funerals were supposed to be sad. I thought people wore black and talked in soft voices. But here—in Abuela's house in Cartagena in Colombia—people whose Spanish I couldn't understand took out their wallets or their phones and showed me pictures of Abuela. Told stories. Someone switched on the radio. "¡Chin-chin!" people said as they clinked their little glasses filled with a Colombian drink called aguardiente. They laughed and then they danced. They danced the cumbia right here in the living room.

It was really something, just like Cameron said about life.

Now glasses and plates are scattered like the leaves in the fall. While Big Eddie sleeps, Nita polishes silver trays and shines the windows. She picks up the cigarette butts left under the lemon tree. I try to help, but she swats the air like I'm an annoying fruit fly.

"No te preocupes, Tito," she says.

Through all this, Big Eddie sleeps on the couch.

"Big Eddie," I say, shaking his arm. He can't spend all night on the couch. "You should go to bed."

He slowly opens his eyes. "Tito," he says. He was one of the people drinking aguardiente, and his breath smells like black licorice. "We're going fishing tomorrow."

I tug him to his feet. "That's okay." I gave up all hope of going fishing in Cartagena. "We don't have to. I understand." Mama told me not to be a burden.

"I'm sorry we haven't gone yet," he says, his voice thick.

"You need to practice for your competition, right?"

I'm surprised he remembered.

"Yes," I say cautiously. I have too many feelings bumping around inside me. Hope, sadness, excitement. It's as if a bunch of clumsy fish are competing for the best spot.

"Well, we should go fishing," Big Eddie says, and then he closes his eyes.

Nita clangs dishes in the kitchen, but it doesn't stop my brother from collapsing on the couch again. He begins to snore. I give up. I take out my phone. Cameron hasn't messaged me back yet, but I text her anyway.

My brother is taking me fishing. On. The. Ocean. I will be ready for the tournament.

Two days after Abuela's funeral, Big Eddie finds a beautiful boat and also a man—who's not so beautiful—to drive it. The fishing boat at the wharf is bright red with a white stripe and has two motors hanging off the back end, and a shiny chrome railing runs along the pointy front. The whole boat is spikey with the fishing rods that are waiting for me. The man, whose name is Johnson, has skin like the sole of a shoe, and he's missing a pinkie on one hand. He wears the dirtiest cap I've ever seen, and a T-shirt with so many holes that it looks like Swiss cheese.

Big Eddie helps Johnson with the gear, and at last we're off. From my perch on the low curved bench at the front of the boat, I watch the waves. I experiment with standing up. Swaying with the rocking, I head to the back of the boat, where rods with shiny reels are lined up next to different-size nets on handles of varying lengths. The sight of all that gear makes me so excited, my arms and legs won't be still. I circle Johnson, who stands at the center console, his eyes squinting as he pushes and pulls levers until black plumes of smoke burp into the sky. I return to the front of the boat, then to the rods again. While I pace, Big Eddie is sitting calmly on the bench and barely seems to notice as Johnson revs the engine and we speed out beyond the bobbing heads of swimmers. I stop pacing for a moment, realizing I actually feel happy right now. But I shouldn't be, should I? The boat careens, and I knock over a stack of buckets like the one that held the leeches. Big Eddie asks if I'm okay, and then he lets a small smile escape his lips while I gather the buckets. I get myself upright and inhale the leftover stink of fish and guts. It's wonderful. I want to drive a fishing boat when I grow up.

Warm ocean water sprays my face as we head toward the horizon. Behind us the beach becomes a thin brown line, and the houses in Abuela's neighborhood are nothing but toy blocks.

Big Eddie looks out at the shoreline and takes a deep breath like he's trying not to be sad, trying to think of other things. "El Castillo." He points at something large and gray on a hill.

"What?"

"Castle," he translates.

There's a pattern across the top of the structure that looks like the Lego castle that Liam and I once built with bright orange and green and blue bricks. I wonder who plays with those Legos now.

"El Castillo San Felipe is five hundred years old," my brother explains. "A fort. That's how our people defeated the British. If it weren't for El Castillo, all of South America would be speaking English now."

I think of all the Spanish words I know, and all the ones I don't. I sort of wish the fort hadn't been quite so successful.

"When I was in school, we visited the castle all the time," Big Eddie tells me. "We came on excursions—what do you call them?"

"Field trips?"

"Right. We took a field trip there every year, all the kids in our uniforms. It was always hot. But in the tunnels, nice and cool. The tunnels run through the fort and let the soldiers get from one part to another. That way they could surprise the enemy," Big Eddie says. "They built channels in the stone. Poured boiling oil on the attacking soldiers to burn them. Pretty creative, right?"

"Gross. That's terrible." I shudder. The waves jiggle Nita's scrambled eggs in my belly. Maybe I don't want to drive a fishing boat.

"Abuela," Big Eddie says, his voice catching on her name, "she used to say that no matter what it is, it's important to know your own history."

If hot oil is part of my Colombian history, I guess it's good to know. But it seems like the more I know, the more I *want* to know. Like, how did they ever think of the idea of hot oil? How did they heat the oil? What happened to the people who were burned? I wish I had my encyclopedia. I wish my encyclopedia had all the answers.

"Look." Big Eddie is pointing again, this time away from shore. In the distance a shape shifts from black to gray against the turquoise of the sky and water. "Do you see the ship?"

I nod. It looks just like a boat I used to play with at the lake.

"And under the water, there are shipwrecks. English ships." My brother stands like he's got a sword in his hand again. "Pirate ships."

Castles and pirates. These weren't in my encyclopedia or in the books I read for my school report about Colombia. It seems like there's always more to every story if you look close enough.

Big Eddie lowers his voice. "And dead bodies." He reaches out and grabs for me, but I scoot away. "Ghosts, probably."

"Do ghosts swim?"

"Sure, why not?"

I laugh. "What about fish?"

"Fish! ¡Hombre!" Big Eddie cries out like he forgot why we're here.

The boat skims the waves, leaving white foam in its wake. The castillo gets smaller and smaller. Johnson slows the engine until the churning waves smooth into a lulling rock-ing. He rummages through a plastic bin on the floor, and he and Big Eddie pull out jiggly silver-and-red octopus-like lures—brightly painted creatures that sparkle with treach-erous hooks—and spools of line that glimmer in the light.

All the tools to catch a fish. Everything is so much fancier than the stuff in Papa's fishing tackle. His lures are broken and faded, and his hooks are rusty, a reminder of how long he's been gone.

I kneel on the floor of the boat and lean over the side, resting my chin on the railing. The water is a swirl of gray and blue and white. Even though I can't see them, the fish are down there. Dozens of them. Hundreds of them. The one I am going to catch is down there. What if a fish jumps out at me?

The boat lurches on a wave, and my stomach swirls unpleasantly for a moment.

After Johnson laces line through the guides on the rods, he shows me how to grip the handle. This rod is much longer than Papa's. Big Eddie's line dances in the ripples of silver water, and I jiggle my own line.

We don't catch anything at first. Johnson lies on the floor of the boat and puts his dirty cap over his eyes like it's nap time. Siesta.

Big Eddie stares at the waves, barely paying attention to his line. His eyes are clear, the most alert they've been since Abuela died. Something is making him calm. Maybe it's the boat or the ocean or—maybe it's me? He's quiet but in a peaceful sort of way. That's how I feel too, both of us with our rods and the ocean and the sun and the two of us not talking.

Except. I have so many questions.

"Why did you change your mind? About fishing, I mean?"

"I wanted to catch some fish, Little Eddie."

I don't remind him that I want to be called Tito now. "But you didn't want to go before."

"Well, I can't let you go back to Minnesota without you fishing in the Caribbean, hermanito."

His voice is distant, quiet, like it's coming through a bad phone connection. I'm glad he's coming home with me, but I wonder if he's sad to leave Cartagena. Colombia may not be my home, but, I realize, it's his. The only home he's ever known.

"Besides, Abuela wouldn't want me to change my plans. Taking you fishing was one of them. And me going to college in the US was her dream for me. And she wanted me to look out for you."

I remember the twin photos—the one at home and the one in Abuela's album—of Big Eddie, Eduardo Aguado León, and the fish.

"What was it like going fishing with Papa?"

Big Eddie is quiet like he's thinking very hard. Seawater sprays in his face and moistens his cheeks. "I'm not sure we ever went fishing."

But I know he did. I saw the picture. The evidence. Abuela has a copy in her photo album. I have one at home in the X-Y-Z volume. Does he not remember, or is he lying? I look at him, but he's squinting into the horizon.

"Tell me what you remember about him," I say instead.

"He was tall and had a crazy mustache like an old man."

"I remember the mustache too."

"Like Juan Valdez." Big Eddie laughs.

"Who's Juan Valdez?" I ask. That's what Mason Schmidt said too.

"The coffee guy? You know, the one they use to sell Colombian coffee to Americans."

"You mean the drawings in coffee ads?" On a bag of coffee beans in Mama's kitchen, a man with a mustache like Papa's wears a poncho and rides a donkey. I've seen plenty of mustaches here and even a donkey, but no ponchos. I suppose it's pretty hot in Cartagena.

"Eso," Big Eddie says. "Sometimes it's a drawing and sometimes it's a photo of an actor who plays Juan Valdez."

"Is he real?"

"What's real, Little Eddie? They made him up to help sell coffee. Sometimes you can use people's wrong ideas about you to get them to do what you want."

Big Eddie pulls his line in and changes lures. He says something to Johnson, but the boat driver doesn't move from his spot.

"I'm sorry I didn't take you fishing," Big Eddie says, casting his line back into the water. Big Eddie reels his line and lets it out. "Antes."

"Awn-tess?" I repeat. "What does that mean?"

"Antes. 'Before.'"

I frown. Big Eddie means before Abuela died.

We let our lines dance some more. Then I ask, "You know that ghost you told me about?"

"The one I saw when I was a kid?"

"I think I saw a ghost. A woman with long black hair. On the patio."

Big Eddie is silent.

"I think it was Abuela. She blew me a kiss."

Then Big Eddie laughs so loud, I almost drop my rod. "It was definitely Abuela." He's laughing, but it turns into something choked, almost like crying. "I told you Colombia is a magical place. And you're a pretty magical kid, Little Eddie."

"Hey, call me—" Suddenly the shaft of my rod bends and I feel an enormous tug. "What—"

"You got one!" Big Eddie pulls in his own line, and his rod clatters to the floor of the boat. "¡Ándale!"

My rod is yanked into an arc. I lean forward. Something is pulling; something is caught.

"Reel it in!" Big Eddie shouts.

Johnson's nap is over. As I crank, the boat driver gets the net ready. This is what I've been waiting for.

"Don't let go." My brother doesn't have to remind me.

"No way." This is my last chance to catch a fish in Colombia. I pull, and it feels like something's alive on the other end of the rod. I mean, I know there *is* something alive there, but it feels like maybe more than a fish. It's like something or someone dancing and doing flips, someone who's really living.

The fish leaps and drags. The water looks like a pot boiling on the stove. My arms tug on the rod and are more tired than the time we had to climb the rope in gym class. But I'm not letting go, not now, not after all this time waiting for it.

"Do you want me to do it, hermanito?"

"I got it." I angle my shoulder so he can't grab the rod.

"Okay, now pull it in," he instructs.

My brother watches as I pull and the rod bends even farther.

There, beneath the surface, I spot something silver, then green, then white. The ghost of a fish appears and disappears as it tries to swim into the safety of the depths. Maybe it's trying to drag me down with it.

Then, like magic, the fish surfaces as the sun breaks through the low clouds. I pull until it's half in, half out of the water. Johnson leans over the side of the boat with the net. The fish's eyes bulge with surprise like it can't believe how blue the sky is. Its nose is blunt like it ran into a wall. The top fin is ruffled turquoise.

"Now let out the line," my brother says. "You want to wear him out."

I let out the line.

"Nice job."

Then the fish arches into the air like a rainbow. It's flying. It's back in the water. It's swimming again. The line twangs, and I pull.

Pull it in, let it out. Reel it in, relax. These are the things I will remember when I compete in the Fourteenth Annual Arne Hopkins Dock Fishing Tournament. That's when everything will work out all right.

Big Eddie is shouting and Johnson is muttering in Spanish, but I'm concentrating on the dance I'm doing with the fish. Forward, sideways, backward. I am dancing the cumbia with the fish. It appears above the water, one last gasp of hope. The line jerks suddenly. The fish swims, it flies.

And then there is nothing.

We all watch as it slips back into its own underwater world. The fish—my fish—has gone home, just like Big Eddie and I will go home.

My rod is empty, the line swinging over the sea as if there never were a fish.

21

BIG EDDIE AND I are on the Avianca Airlines flight heading back to Minnesota. He's in the middle seat. I'm at the window. I try to take up as little space as possible, to be quiet like him. To not be a burden. I think of that saying: a fish out of water. I bet not even a fish out of water feels the way I do. One minute I'm in Minnesota, the next I'm in South America, and now I'm thirty thousand feet in the air. I feel like I got caught and dropped into some guy's bucket and then released into a new lake.

My brother flips through a car magazine. He makes me think of one of those zillion-legged bugs that wake up at night and hide when you turn the lights on. Big Eddie was awake on the boat, but now he has scurried away. Maybe because I lost the fish. No one else caught a fish, and we returned to Abuela's quiet and empty house with nothing to show for our expedition. What if I had caught that fish? Maybe Big Eddie wouldn't be so quiet now.

"Hey, Big Eddie," I say. I can tell he's not reading, because he turns the pages so quickly, a couple of them rip.

When he looks up, I realize I don't have anything to say. I feel the lump in my pocket. He hasn't seen Papa's medal. "Can I show you something?" I ask.

He doesn't answer, so I take that as a yes. I pull out the medal.

"Look what I found at our old apartment. When we were packing."

He lays the magazine in his lap and takes the medal from me. He studies it, turning it over and over as if it might change. He runs his fingers along the engraved letters: *Eduardo Aguado León*. He puts his thumb over "León." Now it says *Eduardo Aguado*. His name. Almost my name.

"From a fishing tournament?"

I nod. "I found this in a box, an old box when we were moving. And it turns out the same contest is at Lake Madeline this year. My friend and I are already registered. We're going to win. But we—" I take a breath. He's still turning the medal over and over. "We maybe need your help. We don't really know how to fish."

He shifts in his seat like he's uncomfortable. "You know how to fish, Little Eddie," he says.

"Not really," I say. If I close my eyes, I can still see my fish slipping into the Caribbean Sea. "Will you help?"

"You were the one who caught the biggest fish. The biggest."

"But I lost it. If I'm going to win the tournament and get a medal just like Papa's, I can't lose the fish."

A cart towering with bottles of water and juice rattles up the aisle toward us.

Big Eddie hands the medal back to me. "You'll do great. Besides—" He's interrupted by the flight attendant and orders Cokes for both of us. Even though I don't really want a Coke, I like the way he takes care of me. He pulls down the tray tables in front of our seats. I don't know if he was going to promise to help me fish, but all he says now is, "Set your cup here."

Instead of doing like he says, I take a sip. And as I do, the plane bangs. It doesn't exactly feel like the plane is going to crash, but it doesn't feel good.

And now I'm covered in Coca-Cola.

Big Eddie looks at me, brown and sticky, and shakes his head like I'm a huge disappointment. Or like I exhaust him. He raises his finger to flag the flight attendant, and when the woman gives us a stack of napkins, I try to blot my jeans and T-shirt, but the sticky stuff has already soaked in.

"I'm a mess," I say. I can't catch a fish, and I can't even drink a Coke on an airplane.

"Oh, Little Eddie . . . ," Big Eddie says in a tired voice that drifts away into silence. He shuts his eyes.

The flight home feels longer than the flight to Colombia. I nap. I eat the meal that comes in a package with miniature dividers between the chicken, rice, and plantains. I read a few pages from the C volume. Cactus, calendar, canoe. After we change planes, I read a few more. Cholera, condor, crystal. Then I shut my eyes, try to sleep, but I can't.

The closer we get to the Minneapolis–Saint Paul airport, the grumpier Big Eddie becomes. And by the time we land on the tarmac, I'm just as grumpy as he is. I'm mad that he won't talk to me, and I'm tired, miserable, covered in dried and sticky soda, and ready to be home. We're surrounded by exhausted-looking mothers with crying babies, businessmen in rumpled suits, tourists coming from Disney World—people who don't know that the world has changed.

I picture Abuela's empty house. The bedroom with the green curtains. The tree in the courtyard and the lemon hidden in my suitcase. The white tile floors that Nita will mop while she looks after the house until Big Eddie decides what to do with it. Is the ghost—Abuela as a young woman—wandering from room to room, sipping juice the color of sunsets, trying to get used to the idea of not being alive anymore?

My throat feels like a chunk of papaya got stuck in it. The woman standing in front of me has a white fuzz in her ponytail. I want to pull it off. I need to pee. I want to change clothes. I need to do something.

I want to cry.

22

THE NEXT MORNING the smell of Mama's pancakes lures me into the kitchen.

"I'm so happy to have you back home." She loops her arms around me and smacks my cheek with her lips about a million times the second I walk in. "I made breakfast for you two." She's as sunny as the summer morning.

I know she's trying to be cheery for Big Eddie, who is already at the table slumped over a cup of coffee. If Mama is the sun, my brother is a black hole. On the drive home from the airport last night, he didn't say much other than commenting on the strange smell coming from the Honda's engine. He didn't talk about the flight. He didn't answer Mama when she told him about orientation at the university and a potluck dinner they're having for new international students. He didn't even talk about Abuela. *I* wanted to talk about her, about Colombia. I wanted to say, *Remember when we danced the cumbia in the living room? Remember when we rode the motorcycle? Remember when we took Abuela to the beach, Big Eddie?*

I showed him the room Mama and I painted the color of sand before I left for Colombia. "Look. We found this dresser in the alley. This can be your desk. And this is a new bed."

I bounced on it to demonstrate its comfy-ness, but all he said was, "Great," in a flat voice. He plopped his suitcase onto the floor.

"I'm so tired," he said, and closed the bedroom door, shutting me out.

"Can I have coffee?" I ask Mama as she flips pancakes.

"You don't drink coffee, Little Eddie," she says, and squeezes my chin.

"But Colombians drink coffee! Can I try it?"

"You're a Colombian boy now? Juan Valdez?" she asks, but she fills a cup half full of coffee and the rest with milk. The coffee isn't hot, but it tastes like Abuela's house smelled.

Mama sets a stack of plates on the counter next to the pancakes. "Help yourselves."

"Do we have any fruit?" I ask. "In Colombia we eat fruit for breakfast."

She raises one eyebrow. "A few strawberries, maybe. Check the fridge."

Strawberries are not the same as a plate of papaya. And serving myself buttermilk pancakes is not the same as having Nita place eggs and arepas in front of me.

Mama watches Big Eddie drown his pancakes. "Think you got enough syrup on those, mijo?"

"We don't have maple syrup in Cartagena," my brother says.

"There's no syrup in Colombia," I inform them, remembering the article I read in the L-M volume last month before the trip.

"I remember that," Mama says, pouring syrup on her own pancakes.

I'm annoyed that she remembers not having syrup and that she's calling him "mijo." After all her not talking about Colombia, not talking about Papa, why is she suddenly remembering things? Everything about Colombia should belong to me, not her. I'm the one who got stung by a jellyfish and ate mango and saw a ghost. I'm Colombian, not her. Big Eddie and I are the ones who just got back. We are the experts.

Big Eddie dumps more syrup onto his plate. "Minnesota has the most delicious maple syrup," he says with his mouth full.

"That's because of the climate," I say. Mama might know stuff about Colombia, but I know about maple syrup. "Maple trees don't grow in South America. They need the cold. Changing seasons. Something about a break—like, a rest before they can make syrup. Or sap. Or whatever. . . ." My voice trails off. I'm not completely sure.

"You sound just like your dad," Mama says. And suddenly I don't feel so annoyed anymore. I stop talking about maple trees and listen, really listen. "He loved the seasons here. The tulips at the Peace Garden, swimming at Lake Madeline, walking in fall leaves along the river. Even scraping ice off the car. He loved all the changes."

Mama is quiet after sharing that memory, like it used up all her energy, and Big Eddie is shoveling pancakes into his mouth as if they'll keep his sadness away. In the silence of the kitchen, I squint out the window at the summer sun and wonder what changes will come next.

After breakfast Big Eddie stays in his room all day. He's like a deflated ball. A flat basketball that doesn't work like one anymore. It's as if, when my brother left Cartagena, he left something behind, some part of him that makes him Big Eddie, a part of him that makes him Eduardo Aguado.

"Let him be," Mama says that night, after I help her with the dinner dishes. We stand in the living room looking out the front window. The sun makes strange shadows out of the linden trees.

It's weird how everything looks exactly like it did before. Antes. At the same time, it all seems different. I see the familiar brown house across the street, Mama's car in the driveway. But there are no lemon trees. There is no ocean. No small children waiting to get me into trouble. Not even Cameron, who hasn't texted me since I told her I was going fishing.

"Big Eddie wasn't like this in Colombia," I say.

"Some people need to grieve by themselves," she says.

"Even right after Abuela died, he wasn't like this."

"Being sad—grieving—isn't something that happens once and then it's over. It can leave and come back in different ways."

Maybe Big Eddie's grieving is like the fish I didn't catch, flying out of the water and then back in. I think of the photograph of Big Eddie and Papa and the fish still tucked in the X-Y-Z volume of my encyclopedia, its twin still in Cartagena.

"Do some people lie when they're grieving?" I ask. Maybe my brother lied about fishing with Papa because he's still grieving. Because he's sad.

"I suppose," Mama says. "They might."

We both stare out the window even though there's nothing very interesting out there. I think about that day in the hospital when I was four. I wasn't sad. I didn't grieve. I guess I was too little.

Mama inhales like she's about to go take out the trash or change the sheets or pay some bills. I don't want her to leave. I like her standing by me, close but not quite touching.

"How did you grieve?" I ask.

She's silent at first. There's hot pressure behind my eyeballs.

"You probably don't remember since you were so little, but I talked to you a lot. Big Eddie came to visit a couple of times, and it was wonderful to see him and to take care of both of you. It helps to do regular things."

Maybe that's why she seemed like she was about to go do housework. Regular things. What's a regular thing for me to do? For Big Eddie?

"Would going fishing help?" I ask.

"Not for me." She laughs. "But maybe if you love it as much as your dad did."

I stop breathing for a moment.

"I'm glad you're using his fishing poles," she says, smiling.

"They're called rods," I correct.

She moves closer, and now our shoulders are touching and I hug her, lean against her, and we're both crying.

Tears, I know from my encyclopedia, come in three different types. There is the kind that keeps our eyeballs from drying out. There is the kind that happens when we get sand or salt water in our eyes. And then there is the emotional kind, the kind that happens when we're happy or sad. No one really knows the purpose of those tears, but people do know that only humans cry when they're sad. Fish don't have tears. I wonder if that means they're never sad.

Mama backs out of our hug. She looks at me like she's seeing me, *really* seeing me, like she's seeing that I'm older, that I understand more. I feel proud but also scared. I don't know if I want to be old enough to understand things.

Still looking at me, she says, "We could have gone to Colombia and stayed with Big Eddie's abuela after your dad died. But I couldn't be there. I wanted to be around his things. Our memories. And you."

I nod and squirm a little until she lets go of me. I plop onto the couch and pull at a few strands of fibers in the upholstery.

"Did you cry a lot?" I ask.

"Of course." She makes a half laugh and wipes her eyes.

We hear the creak of Big Eddie's door opening. We both hold our breath, wondering if he's going to come out.

When the bathroom door closes and the water runs, I

ask, "How long does it last? The crying? The sadness?" I know it's selfish, but I want to know if Big Eddie will be okay by the tournament.

"Oh, Little Eddie. I cried for many months, years. Now I'm sad when I think of your dad, but I don't cry so much anymore." She puts her arm around me and squeezes. A sad squeeze. Somehow that makes me feel sad that I'm not sadder. I'm sad about not having a dad, but I don't really remember him, and so I'm not sad like Mama. And I'm sad about Abuela dying, but not sad like Big Eddie. Sometimes the hardest part about not remembering someone is not knowing how to grieve them. When I think about Papa being dead, I don't feel like crying. Because of this: me and Mama side by side. And even though he's shutting his bedroom door right now: Big Eddie.

"Not everyone cries," she says. "Everyone grieves in their own way."

23

THERE ARE ONLY two more days until the Fourteenth Annual Arne Hopkins Dock Fishing Tournament, and I'm still trying to let my brother grieve in his own way. Which means we haven't gone fishing.

All week since coming home from Colombia, he's been moody and strange. He doesn't seem sad now; he's mad.

It's like living with a ghost.

After the first night, he must have gotten tired of being in his room, because now he goes out all the time. Maybe he just wants to do regular things, like Mama said. Tonight I sat on his bed and watched him get ready.

"Let me teach you something, Little Eddie," he said, filling his palm with sticky blue gel and smearing it on his head. "You got to get the hair just right."

"I don't think that would help me." My hair is so

straight, when I smooth it back, I look like Dracula.

He combed his black hair until it stuck up like frosting on a cupcake.

"What's the point of all this?" I asked, squeezing a drop of gel into my own hand.

"The ladies." He winked at himself in the mirror.

I used my fingers to spread the gel onto the ends of my hair, still not sure if I was doing it right. "How do you know if you like a girl?" I asked in a casual, off-hand, just-wondering sort of way. Not that I like anyone. Not that I was thinking of anyone in particular. Just curious.

Big Eddie reached over and combed through my hair. He patted the top of my head when he was done. "You just know."

That was not helpful.

"Do you want to go fishing tomorrow?" I asked, changing the subject as quickly as I could.

"Maybe. Or the next day."

"But the tournament, the one I told you about, it's on Saturday. At two."

"Vale," he said, spraying cologne onto his chest. He held the bottle up as if he were about to spray me too. I shook my head. "We'll go. I promise."

Big Eddie smiled. It was still his sad smile, though. A smile that made it look like he was pretending to be happy. I thought of what Mama said about grieving.

I pictured the fish leaping out of the water and back in.

· ✳ · ✳ ·

At night when my bedroom door is closed but the lights are on in the hallway, a thin line shines underneath. The sliver is like a lightsaber. In my room in our old apartment, I believed it really *was* one, that it protected me from monsters and ghosts. Goes to show you how dumb little kids are. Because I know that nothing can really protect you.

Tonight I'm looking at the lightsaber in my new bedroom and listening to Mama and Big Eddie argue in the kitchen.

"Where have you been?" Mama asks him now, her voice squeezing under the gap.

"Out," he says. Even through my closed door I can smell his cologne.

"Big Eddie, you need to be home by ten or at least check in with me."

I glance at the clock on my desk. It's eleven thirty.

He asks, "Can I borrow your car tomorrow night?"

Listening to the silence that comes before Mama's no, I can feel my brother careening around the corners of Cartagena.

"When you get your international driver's license, you can use my car," Mama says. This is the same argument they've been having since he got here. The only one, actually.

"Don't worry. I won't get stopped."

"Your abuela would want you to be responsible."

"You don't know what Abuela would want, Liz!" The *z* in Mama's name comes out hard, and I flinch.

"Big Eddie," Mama says softly. She has been saying his name this way almost every day since we got back.

"Me voy," he says, and the front door slams.

I throw back my covers and peer through the blinds. I can see the outline of my brother in the glow of streetlights. Where will he go? He has no car, and the buses don't go very far this late. Maybe he'll walk to Lake Mad. That's what I would do.

The next day when Mama gets home from work, she stands in front of us, hands on hips, and asks, "Have you two been sitting around all day?"

Big Eddie grunts from his place on the couch. I don't answer either. We've been watching TV since breakfast, something Mama would never allow if she were home.

"Take him to Lake Madeline," Mama says, removing the big clogs she wears at the hospital and lining them up next to the door. "It's a beautiful day. Get outside, both of you."

When I first found out that Big Eddie was going to stay with us and go to college here, I imagined me not going to Kamp Kids. I imagined us going swimming and fishing, watching baseball on TV, and taking bike rides and bus rides around Minneapolis. He would volunteer to be a chaperone on field trips at school in the fall, and when it started snowing, I would teach him about sledding and ice-skating and make sure he wore two pairs of socks. I didn't imagine that I would end up in Colombia or that Abuela would die or that, when he finally came to Minnesota, he would lie on the couch all day and go out every night.

"Maybe if we could take your car . . . ," he says.

She just shakes her head. "You don't need a car. Besides, I need to take it to a mechanic."

"I can take a look," Big Eddie says. His voice sounds a fraction lighter, and I remember him working on Arturo's Kawasaki KLR in Cartagena. Maybe she should let him look.

But Mama shakes her head. "Take him fishing. Swimming. Something."

"Not now, Liz." He doesn't look at her.

Mama doesn't get mad very often, but this might be one of those times.

"I know you're upset, Big Eddie, but I need you. And right now you need to take your brother to the lake."

"I don't need a babysitter!" I say. I'm mad at Mama for making me sound like a little kid, and I'm mad at Big Eddie for being mad and sad all the time. I'd almost rather be dumped back at Kamp Kids than wait around for him to want to hang out with me.

Big Eddie lurches off the couch. "I'm going out."

"Fine!" I holler after him. I'm so sick of Big Eddie going off by himself. He didn't do that in Colombia. He stayed home, took care of Abuela. He took me to El Centro and he took me fishing. Why doesn't he want to hang out with me?

I grab the remote control and punch up the volume. Mama clatters in the kitchen, angrily washing the plates we've left in the sink all day. Outside, a car drives past, its muffler chugging. I look at my phone. No messages.

No word from Liam after that picture of him with his new family. I texted Cameron, but she hasn't answered, not since I got back from Colombia. I know she's at Kamp Kids during the day, but even at night she doesn't text back.

Where are you? Are you going to fish with me on Saturday?

My texts pile up, one little bubble of unanswered words after another. I'm just waiting, always waiting. It's like having my line in the water and waiting for a fish to bite. But I don't know if there are any down there.

"Can I walk to the lake?" I ask, coming into the kitchen. "I won't go on the dock," I add in case Mama wants to make me wear the life jacket again.

She has her back to me, rinsing a pot in the sink. Out the kitchen window I see the bird feeder with one chickadee, the tiny rectangle of green that should be grass but is actually weeds. Who will teach me to use that push lawn mower in the garage? When Papa was still alive, we lived in an apartment so there was no lawn to mow.

"I wish your brother had taken you with him."

"Yeah, well." I wish he had taken me too. I wish I could get him to go fishing. Not only because I need to practice but also because I remember how calm and peaceful he was on the boat, how excited he got when I caught that fish, how he didn't seem to mind that it got away.

Mama wipes her hands on a flowered dish towel.

"It's still light out," I say. In Cartagena the sun would have set already.

"Oh, all right." Mama hangs the towel on the oven door handle. "Go ahead, Little Eddie." She doesn't mention the life vest.

The shore of Lake Madeline is ringed with trees. Some are so close to the water that they're practically swimming.

Dead leaves and trash caught along the water's edge make the shoreline stink. I kind of like the smell, though. I watch the sun turn the water yellowish-reddish-orange and keep a lookout for purple hair—I can't help myself. Out of the corner of my eye, I see the old man with his cane and shaking head, the one who sits on the bench every day. He looks as lonely as I feel.

Two fishermen on the dock cast their lines and make arcing rainbows of water droplets. I picture the green tackle box and Papa's rods in the garage at home. When a mosquito bites my ear, I turn back.

When I get home, I call out, "Mama? Big Eddie?"

I don't see my brother, but Mama is in her room folding sheets and towels into neat, square piles.

"Is Big Eddie back?" I ask.

She catches the edge of a sheet under her chin and holds her arms out, stretching the fabric taut. "He's out there," she says.

Mama's bedroom overlooks the corridor of yard between our duplex and the neighbor's garage. On the edge of the weedy patch of grass is a red lawn chair that the last family left behind. I peek out the window and see my brother, his elbows resting on his knees.

"Is he okay?" I ask.

"Maybe you should check."

I leave Mama to her chores and creep out the back door through the kitchen. I tiptoe, careful not to let the screen door slam. Big Eddie's back is to me. The tag of his shirt is sticking out. His hair needs a trim.

He doesn't hear me. Or maybe he does, but he doesn't turn around.

And then I realize that his shoulders are shaking like they were during the funeral. His face is in his hands now, and he's sobbing. I stop breathing for a moment and hear a choking sound, deep and dark, coming from my brother.

I take Papa's medal out of my pocket. Big Eddie reminds me of a wall, like the wall that surrounds Cartagena, one that doesn't move, doesn't talk. I wonder if the reason why he's been a wall, the reason why he hasn't talked to me and Mama about how sad he is, is the same reason why I didn't show Papa's medal to Mama. There is so much sadness in our house. I flip the medal.

Heads: I talk to Big Eddie. Tails: I go back inside.

The disc flashes in the air. I catch it and cup it on the back of my hand. The long tail of the fish. I back up slowly. Big Eddie doesn't turn around as I slip back inside.

24

TODAY IS THE DAY. The chickadees' chattering wakes me up. I sit up in bed, reach for the D-E-F volume of my encyclopedia, and reread the entry for fish as if the words will help me win this unwinnable contest.

Mama interrupts me, simultaneously knocking and entering, something she yells at me for. "Big Eddie's not in here?"

I snap the book closed and wave at my bed, desk, closet. I shake my head as if to say, *Obviously.* I hope he's here by two o'clock, when the tournament starts. He's got five hours.

I'm about to go back to reading about types of fish, but Mama pauses at the door. "You really like the encyclopedias, don't you?"

I shrug. Nod.

"I'm glad we kept them. Your dad would have been glad you're using them."

"Papa?"

"He always insisted on reading them to me. All sorts of random facts."

"I didn't know these belonged to Papa." My voice sounds very small.

She raises her eyebrows and runs her finger along the spine of the book in my hands. "I thought I told you. Well, I'm glad you kept them, Google or not."

She turns and pads into the kitchen. She didn't notice Papa's medal on my desk. The smiling fish stares at me. Water runs in the sink. I remember how badly I wanted to keep the encyclopedias when I first found them. Was there some Colombian magic working? Did I somehow know they were Papa's?

I open the encyclopedia again. I read that fish, like frogs and snakes, are cold-blooded. I already knew that. I knew about cold-blooded animals, but I didn't know that my encyclopedia set belonged to Papa. I slam the book shut and glance over at Papa's medal.

You'll never catch me, the fish seems to say.

I hear Mama opening the front door to get the newspaper that'll be waiting on the stoop like it always is.

"Little Eddie!" A shriek from the living room.

The encyclopedia thuds to the floor.

"Little Eddie!"

I bolt out of bed.

"Where—" she yells. "Where's the car?"

· ✳ · ✳ ·

Some days are magical, like when you see a huge fish eat an ice cream cone or when you make a purple-haired new friend or see a ghost. But some days are the opposite. And today, the day someone stole Mama's car, is the opposite.

She's outside in her gray terry-cloth bathrobe and bare feet. Where last night the car dripped on the driveway, this morning the space is empty except for the stains on the asphalt. No car.

"Where's my car? Where's Big Eddie? Did he take the Honda?" She circles the driveway as if the car is going to suddenly reappear.

"Big Eddie wouldn't take the car," I say, grabbing her arm. "He wouldn't." I say it, but I'm not sure it's true. He kept asking, kept bugging her. He's been acting strange. But would he steal a car?

Then, while Mama and I are looking at the spot where the car should be, a basketball lands with a thud in the empty driveway. Mama is still standing there in her robe. I'm in my pajamas. I tiptoe on bare feet around the greasy stain and sharp gravel of the driveway and pick up the ball. Because our house is on the route to the lake, random toys and junk are always ending up in front of the duplex. Beach balls, sippy cups, jump ropes, sidewalk chalk.

I bounce the basketball once and then catch it as Mama goes back into the house, muttering something about Big Eddie.

Then I hear a shrieking laugh, and someone calls out, "Loser!"

Two curly-haired boys on bicycles are shouting. One of them is riding no-handed. Mason and Ivan Schmidt. And there's Alyssa on a bike too, with a beach towel over her shoulder. Behind her comes another girl with a towel.

I stand there with the ball, like a paralyzed squirrel thinking about diving across the freeway to my death. They skid to a stop in front of me.

"Having some mommy time before you go back to your country?"

My face feels hot. "This *is* my country."

Ivan snorts, and a little snot comes out of his nose.

I wish Big Eddie were here. I wish I weren't here.

"How's your throw, spic?"

I toss the ball underhand, but he doesn't even try to catch it. Alyssa lets her bike tumble, and she runs for it, throws it to her brother.

I whip around to go back into the house. But when I finally figure out who the other girl is, I freeze. Short blond hair. Slightly bucktoothed. The purple has been chopped off, but I still recognize her. Barely. She's wearing jean shorts and a stack of bracelets. Her earrings are so long, they brush the towel slung over her shoulder. She doesn't look like someone who's going to win a fishing tournament later today.

"Did you get my texts?" I ask as quietly as I can. "What about the—"

Cameron moves toward me, but then glances at the Schmidt kids and laughs an Alyssa-style laugh that isn't quite a laugh.

"Loser," Ivan repeats, and pedals away furiously, the basketball tucked under one arm. "Come on, guys."

I watch Cameron adjust the towel and align her pedals like she's stalling. Maybe she's giving the Schmidt kids a head start. What if she's waiting to talk to me and we'll be friends again?

Instead she takes off, coasting down the slight decline toward the lake. At the end of the block, she turns back once to look at me. And I'm left alone in the empty driveway.

"Did he say anything to you?" Mama comes back outside holding her phone, more worried about her car than the fact that I may die of embarrassment this morning before I even get a chance to catch some fish.

"Did who say what?" I'm not sure if she heard the Schmidt boy call me a spic. She would be mad if she did. She would track down their parents and embarrass me even more.

"Your brother. Did Big Eddie say anything to you? Was he planning on going somewhere?"

I shake my head, but I'm not really listening. I can still see Cameron biking down the street with those kids. The image stays in front of my eyes like the spot you see after you look at a lightbulb without a shade.

Watching Mama walk to the end of the block in her robe makes me wish she would get dressed. She peers around the corner and shakes her head. No car. She sits on the front step. I slump next to her as she calls Big Eddie's phone. The line rings and rings. Then the automatic voice mail message plays, then a robot repeats Big Eddie's number until she hangs up.

"Are you going to call the police?" I ask. That's what they do on TV shows.

She shakes her head. "He must have the car."

I nod. I'm sure he has the car too, but I don't believe he stole it. He must have needed it for something. Something important. And then I think I know: he's going to help me at the tournament, and he needed to buy supplies. Maybe a new fishing rod? Maybe some special kind of bait you can't get at the neighborhood hardware store?

After I get dressed, Mama tells me to walk to the gas station. The one Big Eddie calls the store. "Maybe he went there," she says.

"Why would he take the car there? We can walk in two minutes." I don't add that earlier this summer she wouldn't let me walk to the lake by myself, and now that she's looking for Big Eddie—who's an adult, in case she forgot—she's fine with letting me go off by myself. It feels like the world has flipped upside down.

"Just go," she says, her voice as hard as concrete.

When I get back from the gas station (where, of course, Big Eddie is not), Mama is in the living room on the phone again. She got dressed, but she's put together an odd combination of frayed, cut-off sweatpants and a pink striped button-down shirt. Just as embarrassing.

"His grandmother died recently," she says to someone on the phone. "The one who basically raised him. So I understand that he's upset, but I thought being here with us would help. What should I do?" She reaches up and smooths a spike of blond hair that stands on end at the back of her head. It pops back up. "What if he gets stopped?" she asks whoever is on the phone. "The cops are always pulling over black and brown kids. And he doesn't even have a license."

I stand very still. She hasn't seen me standing in the doorway. The cops? Brown kids? I'm not sure what that means, but the catch in her voice tells me it's not good. I look at my own arm. Am I brown? If I could drive, would I get pulled over?

Sometimes English words are just as confusing as Spanish ones.

"No ID, either," Mama says. "I checked. His passport is still here. He doesn't even have his passport. Nothing. If the cops pull him over, what will they do?" She sighs and shudders, the sound making my toes curl. It's sad and desperate and nothing like the Mama I know. This is a different kind of sad, a worried sad. A hopeless sad.

"Remember when that happened with Eduardo?" she asks the person on the phone. I think I know who it must be. It's Sarah, Liam's mom, on the phone from New York. She knew Papa; that's how long they've been friends. Will Liam and I be friends that long?

"Eduardo got pulled over by the cops. And for what? For nothing. A brake light, they said. Poor Eduardo spent hours at the police station. And that was after a ride in the squad car— Oh God." Mama hiccups; her shoulders shake. "My Civic needs a new taillight."

First my feet go numb. My knees follow. They buckle and fold. I wasn't worried, but now I remember the news stories of guys getting stopped by the police, sometimes shot, sometimes killed. I sit on the floor, and Mama looks up. I hope she's not going to ask me to talk to Liam. I can't right now. But I see that her eyes are squinty and pink. "Did you find him?"

I want to nod. I want to say: *Yes, Mama. Big Eddie is sitting on the front steps right now.*

But he's not. He seems farther away now than when he was living in Colombia.

"Did you have breakfast?" she says, covering the phone with her hand. "Have a grapefruit."

I don't want a grapefruit. I don't want breakfast. But I sit down at the table and scoop out segments of the grapefruit that Mama cut, even as she worried about Big Eddie. I eat the bitter fruit and pull the medal from my pocket. It makes a harsh clang on the kitchen table. Big Eddie must have taken the car so that he can help me win the tournament. I close my eyes and make a wish.

I open my eyes. I swear that smiling fish sticks its tongue out at me.

25

THE TOURNAMENT starts at two o'clock, so I only have three and a half more hours to get ready. Because, even though Big Eddie is gone and the car is missing and Cameron's hair isn't purple anymore, I have to try. I think of Papa. Abuela. I have to fish today.

Inside the garage the smell of damp cement and musty cardboard tickles my nose. The cartons and junk remind me of Cameron. I kick a soccer ball that has rolled off one of the shelves. I wish I were in Cartagena, in Abuela's yard, kicking the soccer ball to the Paredes neighbor kids. It's funny; when I was there, I wished I were here, and now I'm here wishing I were there. Isn't anyone ever happy where they are?

The soccer ball rolls to the back of the garage. What if Cameron and the Schmidts come back? I pull the garage door closed using the red nylon cord inside. The space is suddenly very dark. The only light comes from the window of the side door, which I see that someone didn't slam shut. I go to close it, but when I do, I walk past the spot in the corner of the garage where the fishing rods are supposed to be.

They're gone.

The green tackle box, the one I left on the floor next to them before the trip to Cartagena, is gone too.

"Mama!" I'm back in the living room, and she's back on the phone.

"Did he come back?" she asks.

"No. But, Mama, have you seen my fishing stuff?"

"Not now, Little Eddie."

Back in the garage, I tear through the shelves, pulling down the same boxes Cameron and I organized. I tip over shovels, and one falls onto the microwave. The fishing gear must be somewhere. It can't be gone.

But it is.

Inside, Mama's still on the phone. I don't know who she's talking to and I don't care. Not now. The tournament starts in two hours, and I have no partner, no brother, and no fishing rod. Maybe, hopefully, somehow, Big Eddie will show up at the dock. Maybe he'll bring new gear.

I listen to the chirp of Mama's voice as I lie on my bed crowded next to all my encyclopedias. Eduardo Aguado León's encyclopedias. Which one should I read? Which one will tell me where Big Eddie took the car? Which one will say if he stole the fishing rods, too? Which one has the answers? The spine of the X-Y-Z volume cracks as I open it. Xerox, yoga, Zanzibar. The photo drops out. There they are. Big Eddie, Eduardo Aguado León, and the fish. Taunting me.

I roll onto my back and hold the photograph up to the light.

"I'm so afraid of what could happen," I hear Mama say from the living room. A strange sound gushes out of her before she goes on. "I would never forgive myself if something happened to him."

I look at Papa's smile in the picture. I look at Big Eddie's boy-face. The boy who helped catch that beautiful, magnificent, enormous fish. The boy who is making Mama cry. The boy who knew Eduardo Aguado León like I never did.

"Those brothers are so much like their dad. Between the two of them, it's like having Eduardo here again."

I take hold of the two top corners of the picture and pull. The thin Kodak paper barely makes a sound as it rips in half, splitting the fish in two, leaving Papa on one half and Big Eddie on the other. As the two pieces fall onto the sheets, my own hot tears follow.

I must have fallen asleep, because my neck is at a funny angle and the sun is bright and hot, streaming through my bedroom window. I hate sleeping during the day. The torn photograph is crumpled under me. And it's one thirty. This is a terrible day for an accidental siesta.

I rush into Big Eddie's room, but he's still not there.

"Mama!" I shout out the door. "Is Big Eddie back?" Maybe he came home just in time to go to the tournament with me. I look around the room. His bed is made but not as neatly as Nita can make it. Piled on the bedspread is an assortment of things from Abuela's house: a gold picture frame, a small clay vase, a book on farming that was in her living room. There's the juice glass from Abuela's bedside table. The chocolatera that Nita used for making hot chocolate in the morning. I look in the little closet, behind the door, under the bed. No fishing tackle. No rods. Big Eddie's clothes are piled on the chair. Jeans, a Colombian soccer jacket, a pair of purple boxer shorts.

"No sign of him," Mama calls back to me. "Or my car." Her voice is scratchy like she took a nap too.

Maybe Big Eddie is going to meet me at the lake. He has to. I'm not sure where he'll park the car, but he'll figure it out. The Fourteenth Annual Arne Hopkins Dock Fishing Tournament starts in half an hour, but I don't care that I don't have fishing rods. I don't care that I don't have a partner. I don't care that Cameron chopped off her purple hair. I am going to the tournament.

Papa's medal is on the desk next to my bed, and I jam it into my pocket.

"I'm going to the lake, Mama!" I call as I pull on my shoes.

"What?" she calls from her bedroom.

"Bye!" I shout. She can't stop me.

Nobody can stop me.

26

LAKE MAD is as busy as it usually is on a summer Saturday. Gray-haired ladies walking, shirtless muscle men running, sleek bicyclists. I keep an eye out for Big Eddie's black hair above the crowd because I still think he might show up. I still think this might turn into my lucky day.

Next to the dock a tent and speakers have been set up. A big sign strung across the tent says, ARNE HOPKINS DOCK FISHING TOURNAMENT. People are wearing green T-shirts with the smiling, fishing fish. I check in at the table.

"Name?" the woman asks me. She's wearing the same green T-shirt as the others and has a pink bandana around her neck. She's wearing a stick-on nametag with "Louise" written in thick marker.

"Eddie Aguado." I want to say *Tito*, but that's not the name I had when Cameron and I registered. It feels like that was another lifetime. Like it was someone else who paid the fifty dollars and signed up two friends. I don't know where my supposed friend is right now, any more than I know where my fishing gear is.

"Is your partner here, honey?" Louise looks like someone's grandmother, and that makes me think of Abuela.

"My partner is . . . around here somewhere," I lie. I have no idea where Cameron is, but I know she's not here. I scan the crowds. What if Big Eddie shows up? "Um, can I substitute a partner?"

"You'll need to check them in if you use a sub," Louise says, and scribbles something on the roster. "All members of the team need to be present, okay?"

"Got it," I say. I feel bad lying to Louise. But I'm going to win this tournament. Or at least compete. I may not have a partner, much less fishing gear, but I'm not going to let that stop me. I'll figure something out.

I walk to the parking lot near the dock. Big Eddie must be here somewhere. I have twelve minutes until the tournament begins. There's some kind of car show going on, and half the lot is filled with boxy old cars like the kind in the movie *Grease*. Some are pink, some are mint green, and a lot are red. Big Eddie would love this. I scope out the regular cars, looking for Mama's Honda. There are three Civics, but none of them are hers. I see a man with black hair and a Colombian-style shirt, but when he turns around, he has a beard and a receding hairline. Big Eddie's not here.

I head back toward the dock and stand on the shore where the boys at Kamp Kids had the lemonade fight. Little kids of all ages are out with their dads, some with grandmas who look like the registration lady. A family of two little girls and a mom bumps into me. One of the girls drops a bottle of sunscreen, and I pick it up. She takes it without saying anything. I feel invisible. Alone.

I stare at the lake. There, at the end of the dock, at the exact place where Alyssa dropped her ice cream—that is where I will catch the winning fish.

Even though I don't have a rod. Or a partner.

I clutch Papa's medal.

Something pokes me in the back. Some clumsy fisherman. I step aside so that I won't get bumped again, but I feel a second poke. I turn around.

"Cameron."

She's got her short hair—which is no longer purple—hidden under a baseball cap, and she's not wearing earrings or bracelets. She lets her bike topple. Under her arm, sticking out and jabbing me, are two rods. In her other hand is a green tackle box.

Papa's fishing gear.

"You?" I say.

She shrugs. "You weren't using it."

I look at the rod she has shoved into my hands. "You stole it? My fishing gear?"

She locks her bike to the sign that says DANGER DROP-OFF and sits on the grass next to Papa's stuff. She's a traitor. She's a thief. I can feel tears prickling my eyes. I'm glad and so angry at the same time.

"You're a thief," I say. I wish I weren't so relieved to have a partner. I wish my brother were here instead of a thief.

She doesn't look up. "It's almost time to fish, Eddie," she mumbles.

"Why would I fish with you?" I spit the words out. I want to be sure she can hear me. "Besides, I'm waiting for my brother," I lie. Even though I know now that he's not coming and it's not true, I say, "*He's* my partner."

Cameron doesn't answer. She's pulling and retracting the line on the rod in her hands, and I wonder who taught her how.

"I don't want to fish with a thief," I say.

"I'm not a thief," she says, her voice so quiet that I can hardly hear. "I didn't steal your gear."

I snort, a half laugh, half sob. I jam my hand into my pocket and hold Papa's medal. What if I hadn't gotten his rods back? What if the tackle box had been gone forever? An empty feeling lands in my stomach. I look down, and Cameron's hand is inches away from my foot. I have a sudden urge to stomp on her little finger. It's just sitting there, small and pink like an earthworm. Like a leech.

"You're a leech," I say instead. "You know what leeches do? They live off other organisms. They don't have their own lives. They're parasites." I inch my foot closer to her pinkie. What if I smashed her whole hand? Would she end up in the hospital? "No one likes leeches."

"Listen, I didn't steal your stuff."

I don't say anything.

"I helped them, though." Cameron looks up at me. "They dared me. All three of them. Alyssa. Her brothers.

They dared me, and I knew your mom didn't lock that door. I knew your fishing gear would be there."

When did this happen? While we were bringing Abuela to the beach? While I was fishing in the Caribbean? While I was watching my huge fish swim away?

"Just tell me why." I make my words sound as mean and as hard as I can. Because if I don't, I'm afraid I'll cry or, even worse, forgive her.

"I don't know," she says. Her voice is smaller than a minnow.

I'm silent, because I'm tired of people not telling me things. Not talking is sometimes the same as lying.

"I needed a rod," Cameron says finally. "My dad wouldn't get me one. I wanted to practice so I could fish with you. So we could win. And I was going to give it all back."

"But you knew, Cameron. You knew it was my dad's stuff."

She doesn't answer at first, and a slippery thought worms its way through my mind. What if I had loaned her Papa's gear in the first place? I think of Big Eddie not telling me about fishing with Papa. What if I hadn't wanted to keep it all to myself?

"Have you ever felt out of place?" Cameron asks. I look at her, but she's staring at the grass like it's the most interesting video in the world. "Like you didn't belong?"

I was the only English speaker at Abuela's funeral and the only kid at Little Tykes Preschool with a dead dad and the one the Schmidt brothers called a spic. I don't even bother saying yes.

"I just moved here, Eddie. After you left, I didn't know anyone. They—Alyssa, her brothers, a couple of other girls—they started being nice to me after you left for Colombia." Her voice is suddenly sharp, as if it was my fault I had to go, as if it was my fault I have a Colombian half brother and a dead Abuela. "Alyssa started going to Kamp Kids, and her brothers sometimes walked us home, and they were all being really nice to me. Made me feel like I fit in, you know?"

"Alyssa? Really?" I sit down in the grass next to Cameron. We both wind and unwind the reels.

"Don't look at me like that, Eddie. She can be nice. It's Mason and Ivan that are jerks. But then they got to talking about the tournament. They remembered your rods. I'm sorry. I told them I knew you, that I knew where I could get fishing gear. I didn't take it, but I brought them to your mom's house, late one night."

I think of the empty bottles that Big Eddie lined up to keep burglars out. I wish I could have protected Mama and my fishing gear like that.

"But I got it back. I made them give it to me."

As she says this, the blare of a horn sounds from the tent. It's two o'clock. We have two hours to catch the biggest fish and win the tournament. Do I want to win it badly enough to fish with Cameron?

"Eddie!" Cameron cries. "Please."

I think of Papa's bronze medal in my pocket, of the missing car and my missing brother. I think of Mama. I've come too far now, and Big Eddie is still nowhere in sight. "As long as you're here," I say, "we might as well fish."

According to my encyclopedia, fish like to hide in the shade of docks on warm summer afternoons. They're trying to find cool water out of the sun, especially bass. That means we have a good chance of catching some today. They can be pretty big, big enough to maybe win a fishing tournament. The trick is getting the right lures, the right temptation.

Cameron and I are not quite next to each other, but we're not too far apart either. I'm standing at the exact spot where Alyssa dropped the ice cream cone. I peer into the water, searching for the monster. Cameron pulls in her line and starts over, hoping the commotion will attract some dumb fish. I wiggle my line, swing it from side to side. I try to make it look like a real, live worm even though it's just a plastic lure. Cameron reels her line in again, so close that it's almost touching the wooden slats of the dock.

I want to stay mad at her, but there's something calming about standing on the dock waiting for a fish to bite. The longer we wait, the more I feel my anger drift away.

And, man, do we wait. We wait and reel and wait and cast. It's like waiting for a friend to text you back. It's like waiting for Mama to tell me about Papa. It's like waiting for Big Eddie to come home.

Another fishing team settles on the dock behind us. They get their rods in and almost immediately pull out a bluegill.

Then I feel a tug. Suddenly I'm in Cartagena, the ocean spray in my face, the pull on the line. The sparkling water and the flying fish. Cameron smiles a half smile like she can't decide if she's allowed. But nope, it's nothing. My floater bobs on the tiny lake waves.

At the other end of the dock two men in army-green fishing vests pull in a tiny silver sunny and throw it back. Guess it's not my lucky day.

Cameron and I pull our lines in at the same time as if we are some well-rehearsed team that's fished this lake for eons. The water drips off the empty line and glistens in the afternoon sun. Droplets form into butterflies that break loose and flutter away.

Or maybe I'm getting heatstroke.

Cameron takes off her cap and wipes the sweat from her forehead.

"Why did you cut your hair?" I ask.

She fluffs the ends. Then she puts the cap back on, backward this time. "Would you rather be a fish or a middle-schooler?"

She doesn't want to talk about her hair.

"A fish," I answer. "Well, a fish far away from this tournament."

"Me too, Little Eddie." She drops her line back into the water.

"It's Tito," I say.

"What is?"

"My name. Call me Tito."

"That's way better than 'Little Eddie.'" She pulls her line out again. "I think a new name is a cool way to start school."

"Will people make fun of me?"

"With a name like 'Tito'? No way." She brandishes her fishing rod like a sword. "You'll challenge them to a fishing duel if they do, Sir Tito."

We hear a shout across the dock as a mother-daughter team pulls in a pike, bigger than two of my hands end to end.

"Did you see that?" I ask.

Cameron slants her eyes toward the successful fish catchers. "Too bad one of us didn't catch that one."

My shoulders slump.

Too bad my brother didn't show up.

Too bad I don't have a dad.

Too bad Abuela died.

"For two kids that know nothing about fishing, we're doing pretty good," Cameron says. She stands up straighter, plants her feet with purpose on the dock.

"I guess," I say as we flick our rods in unison, and her line tangles with mine. We laugh as we yank and pull. "Or maybe not."

Once we're untangled, Cameron asks, "What if we don't win?" There's a flash of something sour in her voice.

"What if?" I say. Loud. Louder than I expected. "Only one way to find out."

We switch our yellow lures for jangly spinnerbait and cast our lines back into the water where the fish must be waiting for us.

27

THE FISH, it seems, were not waiting to be caught by either me or Cameron. She snagged one sunfish, no bigger than her sneaker, but it slipped away. I have nothing. No fish, no medal, no prize money.

"Time to weigh in," a voice calls over the loudspeaker. Most of the contestants have already gone ashore. We head to the registration table to admit defeat.

"Got skunked, huh?" a man in a damp fishing cap says as we wait our turn. Even though I suppose I always knew that winning was a long shot, it still feels like something good just turned into something bad. Like a hat turning into leeches.

Louise in the pink bandana smiles up at us from her place behind the registration table. "How'd it go?" Cameron and I both shrug. Then Louise hands Cameron a red-and-white bobber printed with the fishing fish. "One free for each team," she says. "Come back next year, you two."

"Humiliating." Cameron holds out the plastic bobber after we walk away from the crowd of contestants and their smelly fish. The bobber isn't even a real one, just a toy. "Want this?"

I stop and open Papa's tackle box and drop the bobber into one of the little compartments. I drop his bronze medal in too. I don't feel like carrying it around anymore.

When Cameron and I get to the corner where she goes right and I go straight, she stops. "Eddie—I mean, Tito." She straddles her bike and rests her elbows on the handlebars. Then she says, "I'm sorry."

Neither of us says anything more as a mother passes us. She's pushing a baby stroller with one hand, and with the other she guides a toddler on a tricycle.

"Fish!" says the toddler, and points at the rods. "Pole!"

Cameron and I look at each other. "Rod," we both mouth.

After the family has crossed the street, Cameron looks at me. "I'm sorry," she says again. "I shouldn't have done it."

I'm not sure what to say. I was mad at her, but having someone apologize makes me feel funny.

"I'm not going to make excuses." She sits on her bike seat and then plants her feet on the ground. "My dad says, 'No excuses,' like it's his life motto or something. But there could be worse mottoes, I guess. My mom is nothing but excuses."

Cameron looks down at her Converse and then picks at a peeling Princess Tiana sticker on her bike handle.

"So, I'm not going to be like her. I'm going to be like my dad and not make excuses. I'm just going to say sorry. Again."

I wonder. What if she hadn't made friends with Alyssa while I was in Colombia and what if she hadn't let the Schmidt kids into the garage and what if they hadn't taken the fishing gear? Would we have caught a fish today? Would we have won the tournament? Would we still be friends?

Are we still friends? Do I want to be friends? I think of Big Eddie, wherever he is. What if he doesn't come back? I picture him carrying Abuela to the water's edge in the moonlight, and I know he'll be back. He has to be. Will I forgive him? Will I forgive Cameron?

"Have you ever made a stupid choice?" she asks.

"Sure." Like the little Paredes kids and the aguamala. Another mom passes us, this one with a baby strapped to her back. The baby's blond curls are damp under a little pink sun hat, and her eyes are half-shut. Her head bounces with each of her mother's steps. The baby looks so peaceful, just letting the world happen, letting the forces of nature work on her like she's riding the wave of life. Could I do that?

"It's okay," I tell Cameron. It really is okay. Everyone makes bad decisions sometimes that hurt people they care about but not because they're trying to. A tight coil seems to unwind itself inside my chest. I take a deep breath. Is this what forgiveness feels like? "Are you mad we didn't win?" I ask.

"Mad? What is mad, Tito? I could be mad about a lot

of things. Mad at myself for—for what I did to you. Mad at Lake Mad for not giving us any fish. Mad at my mom." Cameron takes off her ball cap and hangs it from the handlebars. After tucking her hair behind her ears, she buckles her helmet under her chin. "You asked why I cut my hair?" She spins the pedal of her bike. "I Skyped with my mom, and she hated the purple. I told Alyssa about it, and she told me she agreed. She said it was tacky."

"It wasn't tacky. It was cool. The coolest."

Cameron smiles, a real smile this time. "It was, wasn't it?" She salutes like a Boy Scout and then jumps her bike over the curb. I watch her, and my lungs feel like they're trying to leap out of my chest. I hope she dyes her hair purple again, but I sort of like how she looks either way. I may not have won the Fourteenth Annual Arne Hopkins Dock Fishing Tournament, but I got my friend back.

She pedals into the street, and I gather both rods under my arm, gripping the tackle box in the other hand. When I reach the opposite corner, I stop. I set down Papa's tackle box and stretch out the fingers on my left hand. The box is heavy, and the two rods keep slipping. As I stoop to pick up the gear, I hear a noise like an eagle catching its prey or maybe it's like the wind through a lemon tree or maybe it's like someone's heart breaking. I look up.

Cameron is on the asphalt, her bike half under her. She's partially on the curb, like it's a pillow, like she's asleep, like she couldn't wait to get home to take a siesta. Her arm is bent at a funny angle. An old man with almost no hair is getting out of a silver car. The one that hit her.

Someone is screaming, and I realize it's me. I run across the street.

"Cameron!"

She looks up at me. "It's a bad-luck kind of day," she says, and then moans. Tears fill her eyes. "Especially for my arm."

Other cars have stopped, and I can feel someone standing too close behind me. Heat from all the cars' engines radiates, and I'm sweating like I'm back in Cartagena. Even though it's sunny and warm, it's like a garage door has just closed, plunging me into darkness. I squeeze my eyes shut for an instant. The silky smell of lighter fluid from someone's grill snakes through the neighborhood.

When Cameron cries out, I jerk back to reality and kneel beside her. She has a red gash across the side of her face, and there's a drop of blood about to drip down her cheek. "You're hurt," I choke out.

"Something's not right, but I think I'm okay," she says, but she doesn't look okay. Her arm is lying next to her like it's not connected to her body. "Eddie," she says, clenching her teeth through the pain. "I mean, Tito. I was thinking about how we didn't catch any fish. And I wasn't watching. I swerved—"

Someone puts a hand on my shoulder. I jerk it away and whip around.

"You?" It's my brother. Big Eddie, standing in the street next to me. Mama's car is right behind him, its engine purring. "Where were you?" I yell.

"Hello," he says to Cameron, ignoring me. "What happened? Are you all right?"

"I don't think the car actually hit me." Cameron's face is pale.

"That guy's car hit you?" Big Eddie is angry now.

"It was more of a tap," she says. "And I swerved. And, well, my arm."

"Can you get up?"

He helps her stand and then unbuckles her helmet while she cradles her injured arm with her other hand. The old bald man starts mumbling and apologizing and saying stuff about not seeing her, and about kids needing to watch where they're going, and then he's apologizing some more.

"Mister," my brother says, his arm around Cameron, "please stop. I'm going to take this girl to see a doctor." He opens the passenger door of Mama's Honda and helps Cameron in. He gently closes the door once he gets her as comfortable as she can be. "Come," he says to me.

Cameron's ball cap is in the gutter in a little pile of leaves. I don't pick it up.

28

"WHERE WERE YOU?" I ask my brother as he loads the bike, Cameron's scratched-up helmet, and Papa's gear into the trunk, all of it a jumble. Big Eddie doesn't answer, just waits while I climb into the backseat. I want to ask Big Eddie how he could just leave me. How could he miss the tournament? How could he steal Mama's car? I want to ask Cameron why she didn't look both ways and if she's okay. But I'm crying and I'm trying not to, and I can't get the words out. It's funny how you can feel so many things at once and they can all make you cry. Mad. Sad. Relieved. Worried. Cameron's face is pale, but she's half grinning and she keeps saying we didn't catch any fish.

Big Eddie starts the engine, and I take Cameron's phone and help her call her dad. I lean between the seats and hold her phone to her ear. When she tells him she was hit by a car, I can tell he's freaking out, and she has to calm him down.

"I'm okay, Dad." The way she uses the word "dad" makes my throat tickle. "It was more of a scrape than a hit. Really. The guy didn't see me. I'm fine. Well, not my arm. But otherwise I'm okay."

She doesn't look very okay to me. Her arm is already puffing up and turning a strange reddish-purple color.

"My friend's brother is taking me to a doctor," she says, and I like the way she says "friend." "Okay. I'll have him take me there," she says, and ends the call. "He's going to meet us at the children's hospital," she tells me.

When my brother shifts the Civic into gear, I take a deep, shuddery breath. "Mama's so worried," I say to him. "How could you steal her car?"

"Let's worry about your friend, and we can talk about it later."

"We didn't win," Cameron says. "It's a bad-luck day."

"We didn't," I say to Cameron, and then I look at Big Eddie. "We need to talk about it now. And we need to tell Mama. She's so worried." I don't add how worried I was too. "Why didn't you answer your phone? Why didn't you call?"

He pulls his phone out of his pocket and holds it up. "No battery. No charger."

I pull out my own phone, the one from the trip that Mama let me keep, and I call her. "*Where are you?*" she asks. Her voice is tight, like a clothesline strung across a Colombian courtyard.

"I'm fine. But Cameron had an accident." I look over at

her. I do not use the words "car accident." Cameron gives me a weak thumbs-up with her good hand.

"Oh, no," Mama says.

"She's okay, but. Um . . . I'm with Big Eddie. And your car. We need to get her to the hospital."

"Let me talk to him." Her tone is icy.

Next I hold the phone up to Big Eddie's ear while he drives, and Mama's angry voice sounds tinny and distant. I don't need to hear her to know what she's saying.

"I didn't steal the car. I'm not a thief, Liz," he says, his accent hitting the consonants hard. Then he's quiet. He's letting Mama yell at him, sort of like Cameron did when I yelled at her. "It was the radiator." His voice is low. "The radiator. That's all."

In the A volume of my encyclopedia, I read about the automobile engine. The radiator's job is to get rid of all the heat of the engine. It doesn't do anything fancy like power the wheels or put on the brakes, but if too much heat gets built up, that can be really dangerous.

I glance at Cameron, whose eyes are closed. I'm worried that she's in pain, but the corner of her eye is twitching like she's listening carefully.

"The children's hospital." Big Eddie nods into the phone. "Yes," he says. "No," he says. He puts on his turn signal. "No, you don't need to come."

Above the clicking of the signal, I hear Mama's voice but can't make out what she's saying.

"I got it. And, Liz? I'm really sorry." Big Eddie's voice catches on the tears in his throat. "The coolant. I thought . . . It's easy to get a replacement radiator. Cheap. A friend of mine said to go to the junkyard. I called this morning, and they had a good one. So I fixed it. No more leaking onto the driveway. No more stinky smells."

He's silent.

"Sometimes you need to do something as soon as you think of it," Big Eddie says.

As soon as you think of it. Looking out the windshield of Mama's Honda at the Minneapolis tree-lined street in front of us, it's hard to believe that a couple of weeks ago we were bringing an old woman to the beach in Colombia. Because we needed to. And my brother decided to do what he needed to do right when he thought of it.

"You're all I have left for a mother, Liz," he says. Then his eyes flick up to the rearview mirror and he looks at me. "And you, Tito, you're my brother."

The only sound in the car for a moment is the clicking of the left-turn signal.

"But I'm not a child," he says into the phone. "I want to help you. We're family."

The curtain around Cameron's bed in the emergency wing swipes open. A woman with gray hair and Mickey Mouse scrubs walks in.

"Cameron O'Hara?" she asks.

Even covered with a heavy blanket and with one arm immobilized, Cameron manages to bow from the waist on the gurney.

We're at the children's hospital. On the way in from the parking garage, we passed big posters with pictures of smiling children with no hair, sort of like the old man that hit Cameron. These are children with cancer who have had chemotherapy, the medicine that Abuela didn't want to take. Even though it's not the same hospital where Papa was, everything—the smell, the sounds—makes my body feel like pins and needles.

"And who are these two?" the woman asks.

"My friends," Cameron says, her voice less edgy than usual. My mind flashes to the image of her lying in the street.

"I'm Eduardo," my brother says. "I saw the accident."

"I saw it too," I add.

"It could have been a lot worse," the woman says, strapping a black cuff around Cameron's good arm. "Kids on bikes that don't look where they're going and drivers that aren't paying attention. We see some bad accidents here."

I want to tell her what happened and to explain how it wasn't Cameron's fault and it wasn't the old guy's fault and it wasn't anyone's fault. I wish there was a police officer so I could give my witness statement like they do on TV shows.

Instead Big Eddie says to me, "Maybe we should go home." He shifts from one foot to the other like he's trying to get away right now. His hair is sticking straight up in the back. He has a black smear on his ear. Grease from some car part?

"I don't think we should leave Cameron yet," I say.

"My dad'll be here soon," Cameron offers. "You guys can go."

We settle for waiting in the corridor for her dad while the nurse takes Cameron's temperature and listens to her heart. We lean against the wall in the hallway and see a man in navy pants and a pink polo shirt make a sharp left toward Cameron's room.

It's Cameron's dad. When he goes in to see her, we hover just outside the room. He holds his phone to his ear and with the other hand touches the scrape on her cheek. In between talking to what sounds like an insurance company, Cameron's dad starts asking the nurse questions and then starts kissing his daughter while also yelling at her for not being careful.

"Dad," she interrupts. "These are my friends."

Big Eddie and I slink into the room. Her dad looks Big Eddie up and down, takes in his sticking-up hair and his big feet. Her dad's eyes stop for a moment on Big Eddie's blackened hands. I try to see what this man sees in my brother. My brother who stole Mama's car but only to fix it. My brother who drove a stranger's daughter to the hospital but only to help.

Suddenly, as if he just remembered his manners, Cameron's dad is thanking Big Eddie and shaking his greasy hand, and then he's using lots of curse words when we tell him about the old man and his silver car. Then he shakes my brother's hand some more, and someone with a red clipboard brings Cameron a wheelchair just like the one Abuela rode in, even though it's her arm that's hurt, not her legs. After I say bye to Cameron, Big Eddie and I stand in the corridor watching her get pushed through a swinging door to get an x-ray.

"Is she going to be okay?" I ask when we turn to leave.

He nods. "She's going to be fine. And, hombre, she'll have a good story to tell." Then he winks at me. "Is she your girlfriend?"

My face gets hot, probably turns as red as that clipboard.

29

TWO RODS REST on my left shoulder. In my right hand is Eduardo Aguado León's green tackle box. Beside me Big Eddie pulls the old red cooler on its noisy plastic wheels. Inside are two containers of live bait from the hardware store, a bag of ice, and two bottles of root beer. The night on the beach with Abuela feels like it happened a million years ago. And also like yesterday. And last Saturday, the day I didn't win the fishing tournament and Big Eddie *didn't* steal the car and Cameron *did* break her arm, feels like a *billion* years ago.

Big Eddie was right. She's okay. Her right arm is a mess, but she's left-handed, so she says she doesn't mind. She had to spend one night in the hospital for observation, and she texted me a picture of the room. It wasn't anything like Papa's hospital room. It had bright colors and cartoon characters painted on the walls. She sent me a tongue-sticking-out face, and I sent her a winky face.

Big Eddie was right about the car, too. Once he replaced the radiator, it was fine. Like a lung transplant, it brought the old Honda back to life. He popped the hood and showed me and Mama the yellow cap that says "coolant." "And there's the engine block down there and the master cylinder. See how shiny it is? I cleaned up the engine a little." He petted the black plastic hoses and covers and rubbed the gleaming metal knobs and pipes with the edge of his shirt like the car was his baby. "And, see, right behind the grill, that's the new radiator tucked in there."

"You fixed it," I said. It was broken, and my brother did something to fix it. A whole car. And he didn't need twenty-five hundred dollars to do it.

Maybe the tournament wasn't ever about the money.

"Next time," Mama said to him as we all stood around the car, "you tell us where you're going. Little Eddie and I were worried."

"He likes to be called Tito now," my brother told her.

"Tito?"

"Tito." My brother smiled at me.

"From 'Eduardito,'" I explained. "That's what Abuela calls me. Called me."

Mama looked at me and then at him and then at me again.

"I'll try to remember to call you Tito," she said, "but you," she added, turning to Big Eddie, "you can't drive my car anymore—until you get your license." She smiled and put her arm around her stepson, catching me between them so I became the filling in a sandwich.

Then Big Eddie asked, "You want to go fishing, Tito?"

I nodded so hard, I thought my head would fall off.

"First, I have something for you," he said.

I followed Big Eddie into his room. From his partially unpacked suitcase that still smelled like Abuela's house—Colombian laundry detergent and lemons and fried plantains—he pulled out the red photo album. He sat on the bed, and a picture, one that hadn't been tucked into the plastic pages, slipped from the album.

Big Eddie caught the photo before it hit the floor. He held it out to me. "For you," he said. "Thought you might like a new copy."

Somehow, I already knew which one it was. The same photo Abuela had shown me. The photo I had torn and later dropped into the trash. Papa and my brother and the fish, intact, smiling as if nothing bad had ever happened and never would. The fish's golf ball eyes stared at me. I didn't catch a fish like that in Colombia. And I didn't catch one at the tournament. And maybe that's okay. Because I definitely caught a brother.

Now, as we walk to the lake, Big Eddie stops at the intersection where Cameron had her accident. Ahead of us, the lake water sparkles in the August sunlight. My brother turns his head to the right, then left, then right again and looks at me with my fishing rods.

"El pescador," he says. Since he replaced the radiator in the car, he's been different. Maybe his grieving fish is back in the water, swimming away. He's still sad, but not in that silent, mad, scary way. He bought his books and filled out lots of forms for the university program he starts in September. Mama's going to help him get his driver's license. And he's speaking more Spanish to me.

"What does that mean?"

"You, the fisherman." There are no cars in sight, but Big Eddie doesn't cross right way.

"Pess-kah-door," I repeat.

"Eso," he says, and pulls the red cooler over the curb.

When we arrive at the lakeshore, I see that the father and his small child are right where I left them almost two months ago. And the dreadlocks guy with a bucket like the one filled with leeches is there too. The man with the dirty cap has a radio that blares a song about getting down.

"He's scaring away the fish," Big Eddie says after we pass. "Bruto."

"What's that?" I ask.

"Brutos. Idiots. You know, people who act stupid, people who don't deserve your respect."

"Brutos," I whisper to myself. Trying out the word.

We step on the wooden boards, and our footsteps send little waves out into the lake. In my encyclopedia I read about a guy named Sir Isaac Newton and his laws of motion. The third law says that for every action, there is an equal and opposite reaction. Like when Liam didn't answer my texts and then I didn't send him any more messages. That was the equal and opposite reaction—the silence bouncing back and forth between us.

After Mama called Liam's mom back to tell her that Big Eddie and the car were fine, I told her, "Liam hasn't answered my texts."

"Liam and Sarah are busy," she said, rubbing the notch between her eyebrows. "They're busy figuring out their new lives in New York."

"Can people who don't talk to each other and don't see each other still be friends?" I asked.

"Look, Little Eddie—Tito," she said. I watched over her shoulder as she scrolled through the contacts on her phone. "Do you see all those people?" She scrolled through the names faster. "These are people who used to be important to me—important enough that I called them and texted them and emailed them. I sent them letters." She smiled. "But even though I don't talk to all of them anymore, we're still important to each other. Here." She stopped at the name Amy Franklin. "Amy was in the support group I joined after Papa died. I don't know what she's doing now, but she helped me through a rough time. And this one." Mama showed me a contact that was just a first name and an email address. "Tony was the guy who helped us move. He's important too. All the people we meet and all the people we know change us," she said. "Most of them make us better people."

Is Liam one of those people? He's all the way in New York now, but he made me better at video games and better at sticking up for myself and better at being a friend. Maybe even better at being a brother. Then there's Papa. Eduardo Aguado León. Even though he's not around anymore, his name is probably in someone's contact list and they see it every once in a while, and remember him, what he meant to them. I walk toward the end of the dock. Maybe each person has an equal and opposite reaction on another person.

While my brother drops the tackle box and cooler onto the dock, I lean over the wooden railing, looking for fish. The muskies and crappies and sunnies are down there. All the fish I didn't catch last week. Each one of them a possibility. Every time something doesn't happen, it means something else can.

So many possibilities.

30

BIG EDDIE RUMMAGES through the dusty compartments of Papa's tackle box. He holds up the plastic toy float from the tournament and reads aloud: "'Fourteenth Annual Arne Hopkins Dock Fishing Tournament.'" He nestles it back into its compartment. "I'm sorry I missed it."

I'm about to tell him it's okay, to say that I understand, but then something else catches his eye.

"Isn't this yours?" he asks.

Eduardo Aguado León's bronze medal is in the palm of Big Eddie's hand. The smiling fish is looking up at us.

I'm about to reach out for the familiar disc, when I stop, thinking of all the places it's been over the summer—from a beach in Colombia to a small duplex in Minneapolis to a dock at Lake Mad. I think of the photo of the fish with Papa and Big Eddie when he was little and of Cameron and the plastic float in the tackle box and of Mama in our cozy duplex and Liam far away. "You can have it if you want," I say. An offering for my big brother.

Big Eddie turns it over. He rubs his thumb over the letters of Papa's name. Our name. "Thanks," he says, and drops it into his own pocket.

He wipes something out of his eye and then kneels by the tackle box again. Clearing his throat, he runs his fingers through his hair and then paws through the cracked lures shaped like eyeless fish. "These won't catch anything," he says. From the depths of the red cooler he brings out one of the containers of leeches that he bought. He drops the container onto the planks of the dock and takes one of the rods from me. "Okay, ready?"

"Listo," I say. I grab a bottle from the cooler and take a swig of root beer. "What do we do now?"

"We fish." Big Eddie pries open the lid of the container. The leeches squirm in a writhing dance, reminding me of the hat that was a bucket. He reaches in and picks one up between his thumb and forefinger. It wriggles like it thinks something good is about to happen. Then he pierces the leech just behind its head. I look away, squinting into the sun.

"Hazlo, mi precioso," Big Eddie mumbles as he swings the poor little skewered leech over the railing and into the water. He lets out a deep, satisfied breath. "Your turn, Tito."

Tito. The sun on my shoulders feels even warmer.

Big Eddie walks his line to one end of the dock, where the water's deeper. From where I kneel next to the red cooler, he looks calm and happy. I smile as I lift the lid of the plastic container. I'm ready. The leech is slimy and squishy like mud on a beach, but I say my own version of a prayer as I pierce its flesh. It keeps writhing even after it's on the hook. I squeeze my eyes shut and then jab the hook through the other end. I know that the bait has to die in order to catch a fish, but I keep my eyes closed anyway.

They're still closed when I hear a shuffling on the dock.

I smell them before I see them. A scent of stale Cheetos and unwashed socks.

"Look who's here." The hoarse whisper comes right at me.

I open my eyes and turn around. Of course. Mason and Ivan Schmidt. Beyond them, the guy's radio at the other end of the dock blasts a commercial for some insurance company. The jingle is one of those tunes that gets stuck in your head. I glance at Big Eddie. He's moving his line in and out of the water and doesn't seem to have heard them. When I stand up, rod in one hand and container of leeches in the other, the Schmidt brothers are so close that I can see the pimples on their faces and the veins on their pale hands. Ivan Schmidt steps even closer.

"It's the spic."

The word is a dagger.

Across the lake two dogs are having a barking match. Each yelp is louder and more frantic than the last. Big Eddie still doesn't turn around, and the Schmidt boys haven't noticed him either.

"Hey, wetback," Mason Schmidt sneers. "Didn't we tell you to go back to your country?"

And then all the sounds of the summer day cut away. My

ears ring with the silence. My face feels warm, as if instead of Minnesota's August heat, the Caribbean sun were beating down on me. A breeze blows like a night wind in Cartagena. Something in the air reminds me of the aguamala that looks like nothing but can definitely sting.

"Shut up," I say.

Time slows down as Mason moves toward me.

Then, as if Colombia's magic has followed me home, I swear I feel an arm around me like a half hug. Slowly, like I'm moving through water, I look to the right, where Big Eddie still taunts the fish. It's not him. I look to the left. No one. Now I feel the arm shift to a hand on my shoulder, gentle and frail. It squeezes with surprising force as if to say, *You are a strong boy. A strong Colombian boy.*

"Shut up," I say again. It's like my voice—loud and deep and so angry—doesn't belong to me.

Both Schmidt brothers laugh, and Ivan shoves me.

A roar rushes in my ears like a plane taking off. My Colombian blood boils and churns. The muscles in my arms and legs and feet tense. My face is hot, burning like a fire. This is it. I've had it. The weight on my shoulder is firm and comforting, and I am stronger and braver and more powerful than I have ever been before.

As Ivan makes contact with my chest a second time, I yell, "Quit messing with me! If you touch me again, you'll be sorry."

"Oh yeah?" Mason taunts.

I'm still holding my rod in one hand and the container in the other. The pressure on my shoulder increases comfort-

ingly. I look into the eyes of Ivan Schmidt and see hatred
and fear, both mixed together. Mason pulls his hand back
as if preparing to hit me too.

And then, without my really knowing it, I am reaching up,
standing on my toes, making myself as tall as possible, and,
smooth as an ocean wave crested on the shore, I am dumping the contents of the still-open bait container onto them.
The leeches that don't get caught in their hair and in their
shirts and in the crooks of their elbows fall to the dock, and
some slip between the boards to become fish food. Only a
couple of brave leeches have managed to attach themselves to
the pale flesh of the brothers. Both boys are screaming now,
jumping, hopping. Out of the corner of my eye, I see the guy
with the radio watching us. The fisherman with dreadlocks
chuckles at the sight of the dancing and squirming teenagers.

"You know what?" I say, calmly setting the empty container down at my feet. The pressure on my shoulder lifts
little by little, like someone backing away, letting me be on
my own. "You guys are a couple of—"

What are they? Cretins? Dirtbags? Scum?

Racists. Ignoramuses.

The weight of the arm around me is gone now.

I know what they are: they're jerks.

"You guys are a couple of brutos!" I shout even as the
Schmidt brothers squirm and yell curse words.

Down the dock from me, Big Eddie pulls his line out of
the water and looks at the scene like he just woke up from
a dream. His eyes widen at the sight of the leech-covered
bullies. "¿Qué pasó?"

And I realize I'm not on my own. I've never been on my own. Mama, Abuela, Big Eddie.

"In case you were wondering," I say, "this is my brother."

It only takes a moment for the Schmidt boys to scan Big Eddie, from his slick black hair to the shadow of a beard on his chin to his long pointy shoes. I don't know if they remember him from that day on the playground, but he's a lot taller than he was then. Each one of his shoes could fit all four of their feet, and his arms are tree trunks compared to their skinny biceps.

"Brutos!" I spit out the word like a missile, rolling the *r* perfectly just like Big Eddie did. I take a deep breath. "Don't you mess with me again!"

A millisecond later they're running, still pulling leeches off each other. "You guys are crazy!" they shout as they stumble off the dock.

31

AT LAST I HOLD my fishing rod over the dock's railing. The Schmidt boys are gone, but my hands are still shaking. Big Eddie thinks they won't be bothering me again. He says bullies look for weakness and that I'm definitely not weak. Then we laugh again at the thought of the two of them covered in leeches. I look into the water where my little leech will lure in a big fish.

The radio at the other end of the dock is playing something quiet now, maybe a love song. A duck lands along the shore with a noisy splash.

And then there's a tug.

"I feel something!"

"Already?" My brother leans his rod in a notch in the dock's railing and comes to look.

Another tug. An equal and opposite reaction.

Big Eddie helps pull in a good-size perch—about seven inches, he says. The fish flops on the wooden slats. "Nice," he says.

I caught a fish. A real, live fish.

My brother takes hold of the fish in one hand and pries the hook out. The eyes are black and frightened-looking. Blood stains the fish's mouth. The sight makes me glad we didn't catch any fish at the tournament. Me and Cameron weren't ready for this much violence.

"Good work," Big Eddie says, admiring the little fish.

I feel about as tall as a tree. I pull the second container of leeches out of the cooler and cast my line back into the water after baiting the hook. Without closing my eyes this time.

"Big Eddie?"

He grunts. He's moving his line again, trying to make it look delicious to some fish.

"Can I ask you something?"

He squints into the water and then across the lake.

"That picture? Of you and our dad and that fish? Do you really not remember going fishing?"

The question lands with a thud like a soccer ball against bricks. I'm afraid it'll bounce back, unanswered.

But Big Eddie asks, "Do you know why Papa loved fishing?"

"Because he loved fish?"

"No." Big Eddie jiggles his rod. "Fishing isn't about fish."

"It isn't?" I jiggle my own rod, even though I'm not sure if I'm doing it right.

"When I was five years old, I was supposed to take a bus

with my mother to visit her friend in Santa Marta. I begged to stay home. I wanted Papa to take me fishing instead. I told Mami that I wanted to go fishing, not be in some hot and sweaty bus. She laughed and told me to catch her some fish for dinner. So we fished for her.

"We were on a boat like the one I rented in Cartagena. That one was yellow. When my line jerked, I was so little that Papa had to help me hold it. We both pulled and cranked. The fish was bigger than me." As he speaks, I can see the fish in the photograph, its huge eyes and teeth. The broad smile on my brother's five-year-old face, wider than any I've ever seen on him. "The guide filleted it for us so we could bring it home. We would eat like kings."

There's another tug on my line, but I ignore it.

"We didn't know until later that the bus crashed. Two of them. They slid down the mountainside. We were catching the biggest fish you ever saw, while Mami was dying."

Big Eddie is quiet. The radio blasts a song about rolling, and my insides roll too. I don't know what I was doing at the moment Papa died. Was I doing something wonderful? I was only four. Probably back in preschool or maybe with Liam and his mom. I know I wasn't at the hospital. I didn't see him take his last breath.

"Colombia is strange like that. One terrible thing and one amazing thing. Both things at once," Big Eddie says, reeling in his line and then casting again.

Is seeing a ghost a bad thing? Is a hat turning into leeches a good thing? Is Abuela's death after we took her to the beach a bad thing? Or is that all backward?

"Papa said she would have been glad. Not that it made me feel any better. He said she would be glad that we were happy."

Maybe everything has a good and bad side, like heads or tails, and it doesn't really matter which is which.

"Fishing isn't about fish, Tito. Fishing is about being in the moment. Now. Here." Big Eddie wipes his eyes with the back of his hand. "Speaking of now, it looks like you've got another one."

I reel in another fish, this one almost ten inches. I keep catching fish, little ones, mostly sunnies. It's like all the fish I didn't catch last week are lining up to be caught today. By my fourth fish, I brave its accusing eyes and remove the hook myself. It's just as gross as I thought it would be.

Big Eddie loops a stringer through the mouths of the perch and the four sunfish that I caught and slowly lowers them into the water.

"Might as well string these up, leave them in the water. Keep them fresh for dinner."

I'm not sure I want to eat any of these fish. And I'm pretty sure Mama won't want to cook them. But she loves Big Eddie and so she might do it for him. And I love him too, so I might eat them if I have to.

At the railing Big Eddie unbuttons the top four buttons of his guayabera. The shirt is white with light blue embroidery. It's from Cartagena. He wanted me to get one too, but I was embarrassed. I thought he would look weird on the streets of Minneapolis with that fancy shirt, but somehow Big Eddie looks even more like Big Eddie.

I scan the dock and the shore, wondering who might be watching my older brother in that fancy guayabera. I catch a glimpse of purple. Cameron cut her purple hair off, so I know it's not that. Besides, I'm not sure her dad would let her come to the dock so soon after the accident. I turn back to the water.

"Hey," someone says behind me.

There she is. It *is* Cameron. With a completely purple head and matching purple cast on her right arm.

"Cameron?" I can't stop staring. Every strand of hair is purple.

"At your service." Cameron sweeps one arm awkwardly to the right, the other to the left. She bends forward until she's practically folded in two.

"Your hair."

"Yes, my hair. If you are wondering if it's purple, it is. It is indeed purple. I did it myself. Between the hair and the arm—you should've seen my mom's face when I Skyped with her."

"Nice cast," I say.

"Do you like it? All the cool people are wearing them this year. Looks like I'll be starting middle school with the latest fashion accessory. Me with this; you with a new name, Tito."

We laugh, and then she sees Big Eddie.

"Hi," she says shyly. My stomach drops when she looks at him and blushes. "Thanks for everything. At the hospital."

Big Eddie looks up from the tackle, and she turns back to me and smiles. My stomach returns to its usual location.

Then I show her the leeches and tell her about Mason and Ivan, and then Big Eddie teaches her how to murder them. The leeches, I mean. He explains that the fish by the shore are looking for little critters that hang out under the dock, so you have to make the leech look like something yummy.

"You have to think like a fish." Big Eddie snaps the container's lid shut.

"I like the way you talk," Cameron says.

"How do I talk?"

"Like you're from Colombia."

"I am. Soy Colombiano. Just like my little brother. We're both Colombian."

Cameron and Big Eddie smile at each other, and even though no one is actually hugging, I feel like I'm the filling in the sandwich again. I wiggle my line. This would be a really good time to catch the big one.

"Want to try?" Big Eddie offers the rod to Cameron. "Can you do it one-handed?"

"I can do anything," she says, and takes the rod in her left hand. She stands next to me. When the dock sways, our elbows touch. And when our elbows touch, my toes wrinkle. An equal and opposite reaction.

And then Big Eddie erupts in a shout. "Did you see that?" We both look down. "That thing just ate your fish!"

There, in the water, where Big Eddie is pointing, instead of five fish there are now four. Well, five heads and four bodies. The smallest fish has been decapitated—or whatever the opposite of that is.

"Your fish," Big Eddie says, wheeling around and spinning and laughing, "is bait. Espera—let's get the others into the cooler."

Big Eddie dumps them into the red cooler, where they look shocked at the confined space. One minute they were swimming around among green plants and underwater weeds, and the next minute their lives are totally different. Over, actually.

"Wait," Big Eddie says. "Here's what I'm gonna do."

My brother takes my rod from me and loops the line and hook around one of the fish that still has a body. He drops the wriggling thing into the water with a splash and hands me my rod.

We have an audience.

The guy with the radio shuts off his music. A few joggers pause to watch. Two little kids stand with their father, their mouths slack. Cameron, my brother, and I huddle at the railing.

At first nothing happens.

The crowd behind us grows restless.

"Never gonna happen," someone says.

What do we care what they think? My brother is going to help me catch the big one.

"I feel something." Cameron grips Big Eddie's rod tighter.

"Hold on," he says.

Her knuckles whiten with the effort, then relax. "Never mind. It was nothing."

But it's not nothing. We hear a splash. Then there's a pull on my rod, the one with the fish as bait.

I brace my feet against the boards of the dock. "Big Eddie! Help!"

"¡Juepucha! Hold it, Tito."

I wrap my hands around the cork grip. It's black with grime left from my brother and, before him, our dad. I hang on to the handle, and Big Eddie yanks on the rod. The line reminds me of a dot-to-dot: the dock is one, and the surface of the lake is two. Somewhere down deep in the water is the fish—three.

My brother and I both pull. Whatever is down there seems to get more determined to stay there. "Come here," Big Eddie says to Cameron. "Ayúdanos."

Cameron looks at me and back at him. She doesn't know what he's asking. But I do. "Help us," I translate.

She grabs the rod too, even though she only has one hand to do it with. Cameron, Big Eddie, and I are stationed along Papa's rod, each of us gripping and pulling. We are a new dot-to-dot. Friend, brother, me. Together. My worries slip away as easily as a fish off a line.

But this fish isn't getting away. It flies out of the lake. Everything is a blur of water and slime. Thrashing tail. Bent rod. Stomping shoes.

A magnificently ugly fish flails on the dock. It's grayish brown with a mean face. Its scales shimmer, and a rank, prehistoric smell wafts up. A northern pike? Every word I've ever read in my encyclopedias drains out of my memory as if my brain is a leaky bucket. Whatever the creature is, it's big. Bigger than three of Big Eddie's shoes end to end. Or twice that.

And this fish isn't done being alive yet. The front of Big Eddie's white guayabera is now brown with fish gunk, and his arms bulge with muscle. The fish thrashes and bucks like a bull. It makes a squeaking, squawking sound, its mouth opening and closing around the hook.

Big Eddie shouts, "Get me the cooler!"

I scramble to the cooler and drag it to where the fish lies panting on the wooden slats. Big Eddie kneels down next to the creature. Now, it might be hard to believe, but that fish actually lunges at him.

When I first saw the photograph of Papa and Big Eddie and the fish, this wasn't what I imagined catching one was like. My brother reaches around the monster's gills to yank out the hook. The teeth are lined up like soldiers ready to fight.

Then they do.

"The thing bit me!" Big Eddie jumps back. Red blood adds to the stains on his shirt. But he's laughing, panting, shouting. "Damn!" Big Eddie's words come out in a mix of Spanish and English, and I can't understand either but I'm pretty sure there's a lot of swearing in both languages. Cameron's taking pictures one-handed, kneeling in the muck on the dock. Despite his bleeding finger, Big Eddie hugs the fish and leers for the camera. I lean in too, our heads touching. We're two half brothers making a whole picture.

"Help me get this thing in here, Tito."

I shove the cooler closer to the beast.

"You can't keep that thing," someone in the crowd on the dock says.

"No way," the guy with dreadlocks says.

A woman in yoga pants says, "I don't think you're allowed to take it home."

Big Eddie stops lugging the dying fish to the cooler. He looks at the crowd. "Watch me," he says, and grins wider than I ever thought possible.

Big Eddie tosses the smaller fish into the water to make room for the big one. He heaves the northern into the cooler. The head flops awkwardly over one side, the tail over the other.

The crowd parts for us and our fish. Or maybe everyone is done watching the spectacle. The guy with the radio switches the music on again.

Cameron salutes me with her right hand. "You did it, Tito."

"That's a good-size fish," the dad with the little kid says as we pass.

It *is* a good-size fish. Not quite as big as the fish Papa and Big Eddie caught in Colombia. But big enough, maybe, to prove to Big Eddie that Minnesota is a fine place to be, that having a little brother is a good thing. Big enough to prove to myself that I could have won the tournament just like Papa. I reach my hand into my pocket and then stop. I glance at my brother. I don't need a medal to know that I carry a little bit of Papa around with me all the time.

In the fading orange light of late summer, we head home. At the corner, we wave good-bye to Cameron, who salutes with her good arm and then looks both ways before crossing the street. The rods swing on my shoulder. Big Eddie carries the tackle box. Between us, we pull the cooler, the fish like an emperor in a chariot. It feels like the setting sun might hang in the sky above us forever—the summer, the fall, maybe even our whole lives stretched out before us like a vast ocean.

Acknowledgments

Thank you to the early readers who believed in Little Eddie's story, especially my fabulous editor, Amanda Ramirez, at Simon & Schuster and my lovely agent, Thao Le, and the University of Minnesota Press, which published my original Eddie story, "Fishing," in *Sky Blue Water: Great Stories for Young Readers.*

Thanks also to these people and places that were instrumental in some way in the creation of this book: Erik Anderson, Karlyn Coleman, Adrianna Cuevas, Linda and Al Dieken, Nancy Duncan, Renzo Fajardo, Marcela Landres, Las Musas, the Loft Literary Center, the Minnesota Fishing Museum, the Minnesota State Arts Board, Regan Byrne Palmer, #PitchWars, and Jen Vincent.

I am especially indebted to my daughter, Sylvia, who helped me work through exactly what could and should happen in Little Eddie's world and inspired many of his adventures; to my Colombian family and our Cartagena adventures; and to my husband for supporting me in all the possible ways a writer must be supported.

Finally, this is in memory of Sally, my own Abuela.